UNSTOPPABLE

UNSTOPPABLE

Dan Freedman

David Fickling Books

31 Beaumont Street
Oxford OX1 2NP, UK

Unstoppable
is a
DAVID FICKLING BOOK

First published in Great Britain in 2019 by
David Fickling Books
31 Beaumont Street,
Oxford, OX1 2NP

978-1-788450-49-2

3 5 7 9 10 8 6 4 2

Papers used by David Fickling Books are from well-managed forests
and other responsible sources.

MIX
Paper from
responsible sources
FSC® C018072

DAVID FICKLING BOOKS Reg. No. 8340307

A CIP catalogue record for this book is available from the British
Library.

Typeset in 12/19 pt Sabon by Falcon Oast Graphic Art Ltd.
Printed and bound in Clays Ltd, Elcograf S.p.A

This book is dedicated to:
My dad, Brian Freedman
My teacher, Dave Baldwin
My friend, Ugo Ehiogu

14 YEARS AGO

Two newborn babies are lying, side by side, in a cot.
They are twins, but they are different.
A girl and a boy.
The girl was born first, late into the night.
The boy followed soon after.
The girl has light skin and is punching out her arms.
The boy has darker skin. He is quiet and calm.
They clasp one another's hands.
They are one.

Compton Estate

High Street

Chicken Shop

COMPTON AREA

INSPIRED BY TRUE EVENTS

PART 1
FIRST CUT

PRESENT DAY

SUNDAY

Roxy Campbell looked at her watch. The hairdresser would be arriving any minute, but there was still time.

She stared out of the window. From her brother Kaine's room she could look out across the whole of the Compton Estate and down the five floors to the tarmac sports court where he was playing football.

She could see that, as usual, he was showing off. He had just kicked the ball between his opponent's legs and was now taunting that same opponent for not having been able to stop him. Why did he have to be such an idiot? He brought trouble upon himself.

Navigating her way through the strewn mess of

trousers, shorts and socks on the floor, she picked up his right football boot and, using her mum's sharpest scissors, started to make two small incisions on either side of the tongue. They wouldn't be seen, but they would do the damage that she required.

Guilt stabbed her from the inside. But she carried on, picking up the left boot to replicate the damage.

The doorbell went, and Roxy heard her mum answer it and welcome Simone inside. She carefully placed Kaine's boots back where she had found them and left the room.

Kaine had already taken the ball past Rufus Blackstock once, but he went back and did it again, just to show how easy it was.

'You think you can make me look stupid?' Rufus said, pushing Kaine hard in the chest. 'Try it one more time and I'll break your legs.'

'Who do you think you're pushing?' Kaine responded, shoving his rival back with such force that he nearly fell over.

'Leave it, Kaine!' said Alonso Jackson, trying to pull Kaine away.

'He started it!' said Kaine, spitting on the ground and pulling AJ's arm off him as they walked back into their own half. He was still muttering to himself as the game quickly kicked off again.

Kaine immediately called for the ball and watched as the goalkeeper bowled a high throw straight out to him. Sensing Rufus rampaging towards him from behind, Kaine both controlled the ball and turned in one touch before lashing a strike towards the goal with such ferocity that the goalkeeper couldn't get out of the way quick enough.

'How d'you like me now?' Kaine shouted, going right up to Rufus's face to celebrate. 'You're just upset cos you're even uglier than your mum!'

'What did you say about my mum?'

'You heard me!'

'I'm gonna kill you,' said Rufus. 'You're dead. I promise you. You're dead.'

He drew his finger across his neck in a throat-slitting gesture, but Kaine just laughed. He knew if someone said something like that about his own mum, he would go ballistic at them too. He decided to carry on and wind Rufus up a bit more.

'Yeah, mate, I'm really scared,' Kaine said. 'Your mum's more scary than you are. Especially when she tries to kiss me!'

'There,' said Simone, using her own small mirror to show Roxy what her hair looked like from behind. 'What do you think?'

They were sitting on the bed in Roxy's small, but well ordered, room. Roxy nodded at Simone and took hold of the mirror herself to make a closer inspection from different angles. Finally, she smiled.

'It's perfect,' she said, getting up and marching into the living room. 'Mum, Dad, look! What do you think?'

'You look beautiful,' said Samantha Campbell, giving Roxy a kiss. 'I'm just sorry it took so long to give you your present . . . it's just, well, you know . . . Anyway,' she said, looking at Roxy's dad, 'with any luck things will get a bit easier soon.'

It had been three weeks since the twins had turned fourteen, but with only their mum's income to support the whole family, their presents had been delayed. The front door burst open and in walked Kaine and AJ. Roxy immediately felt her body tense up.

'Ha!' said Kaine, seeing everyone gathered by the mirror in the living room. 'Trying to get people to look at your hair so they don't concentrate on the rest of you, Roxy?'

Roxy looked at Kaine. No matter how many times

he was cruel to her, it always hurt. And when it was in front of AJ, it cut like a dagger.

'Go away, Kaine!' she said. 'You can talk! When are you going to get *your* hair cut? You don't look cool, you know!'

'Yeah,' he said, elbowing AJ in the ribs. 'Like she knows anything about cool! Anyway, Mum, when am I going to get my trainers? How come she's got her birthday present, but I haven't got mine?'

'We told you, soon, Kaine!' Daryll Campbell said.

'I'm asking Mum, not you!' said Kaine. 'We all know she's the one paying for it.'

Roxy could see the vein in the side of her dad's neck starting to bulge. She knew it was only the presence of Simone in the room that was stopping things from getting ugly between him and Kaine.

But Kaine was already going, stomping across the hallway to his room. 'Come on, AJ,' he called. 'FIFA. Now. I'm gonna smash you up, boy.'

'Well, I think you look great,' AJ quietly said to Roxy, giving her his cheeky smile before dashing after Kaine.

Roxy could feel herself blushing but did her best to quell it. Especially in front of her dad.

Later that evening, Roxy stared into the bathroom mirror at her own reflection. She wondered what the girls at school would make of her new look on Monday morning.

She missed Jasmine. They had been so close from Year 7 onwards but, since Tochi had come on the scene, they had drifted apart, and the last few times Jasmine had asked her to come to the chicken shop or to have pizza, Roxy had said she couldn't – there was no way her dad would let her eat junk food.

Now Jasmine and most of the other girls had boyfriends, and when they did hang out together as just the girls, they'd stopped inviting Roxy. It made Roxy jealous to see them all together in school, and the fact that they all had boyfriends somehow made them feel older than her, even though they were all in the same year. The only way she knew what was happening in their lives was by following their accounts and looking at their photos.

She consoled herself with the fact that AJ had said that she looked good. But what did he really mean? Was he trying to give her some kind of message?

'What are you doing in there, Roxy?' said her mum, banging impatiently on the bathroom door. 'You know your dad needs to shave his head before tomorrow. There won't be time in the morning.'

Roxy unlocked the door and her dad pushed his big frame straight past her. Sometimes, when she wasn't on the tennis court, she felt as though he barely noticed her. She could see the nervousness in his eyes and sense the tension that was already in his body. Everyone in the family knew that if he didn't get that job the next day, their lives would get even harder.

As he arrived home and put the previous night's dinner into the microwave, Noel Kerrigan, Deputy Principal at Compton Academy, found himself still thinking about Kaine Campbell.

He'd been doing some marking at school, and on his way home had stopped by the Compton Estate to see what was happening. The boys had been playing football and he'd stayed to watch for a few minutes. It wasn't Kaine's goal that he couldn't get out of his mind. And it wasn't the fact that the game had nearly descended into a brawl that he was thinking about right now either – though he would need to mention it to Mrs Buckland.

It was that one touch: Kaine's exquisite, arrogant piece of skill from the keeper's long throw. With each passing day, he was becoming more and more convinced that Kaine Campbell – his Year 9 pupil at Compton Academy – was a natural-born footballer.

He took a swig of his beer and checked the time. It was late, nearly 11 p.m., but he picked up his phone and made the call anyway. It rang out, so he left a message.

'Brian? Noel Kerrigan here, mate. Listen, are you still scouting for Southampton? There's a kid, Brian. He's fourteen. We've got a school match on Wednesday. I think you should come and have a look at him.'

MONDAY

Lying in his bed, Kaine heard his parents and Roxy leave. They all had their busy little lives that they felt were so important. His dad and Roxy would be going to school to use the court there, and his mum would be starting her shift at the care home. Standard. His window was open, so he could hear them traipsing down the steps.

As their footsteps slowly faded away, a feeling of peace and calm finally washed over Kaine. They were gone. At last. He'd had it with all of them. His dad and Roxy's partnership or tennis obsession – or whatever they wanted to call it – weirded him out. He knew that Roxy wasn't the sweet little girl that she liked to make everyone think.

She was way more devious than that, but he was the only one that could see straight through the act.

Meanwhile, his mum may as well not have existed. The only thing she ever did now was work all hours of the day. She hardly ever cooked for Kaine and Roxy any more. She just kept saying that since everything relied on her job, if she didn't get to the care home on time, then there'd be no food to eat anyway.

Now he had the flat to himself, Kaine could breathe. Just knowing that none of them were there made the world a far better place. He checked the time on his alarm clock: 7.04 a.m. He could have another whole hour's sleep and a couple of games of FIFA before he even had to think about getting to school.

And if he was late, who cared anyway? The first lesson was history, and Kaine knew he could get away with whatever he wanted with Mr Hollis. The man never seemed to get angry. The week before, when Mr Hollis was explaining about the Gunpowder Plot and asked if anyone had any questions, Kaine had put up his hand and, with a completely straight face, said: 'Sir, it's not about the plot itself but . . . I had a curry last night and my bum honestly feels like it's on fire now, do you mind if I scratch it?'

Kaine made himself laugh just thinking about it. He knew school wasn't what was going to be important in his life. Only football was. His teachers could waste their time talking about irrelevant facts, but he didn't have to listen.

He turned over and tried to get back to sleep but he could hear his stomach grumbling. What he would do for one of Mamma's home-cooked meals now.

'You are a tricky customer, Kaine Campbell, but I know how to get round you.' Mamma smiled as she produced her world-famous salt fish and cou-cou special.

The sweet smell filled the air, and Kaine could already taste the flavours in his mouth before he had even taken his first bite. A cut of cod, served with cou-cou (which was made mainly from cornmeal), sweet potato, a hard-boiled egg and, best of all, everything drenched in a smooth, buttery tomato sauce, the dish was so good that every time Kaine tasted it, he thought he had died and gone to heaven.

Kaine had been refusing to get his hair cut for weeks, and it had been getting more and more out of control until finally, Remmy – or Mamma as she liked to be called by her grandchildren – had come up with a solution to the problem, just as she always seemed to whenever there was an issue in Kaine's life.

Her proposal had been a simple one, which had been to both parties' satisfaction: one haircut in exchange for one of her trademark home-made dishes from Barbados. She watched as Kaine launched himself into the succulent dish, chewing and nodding vigorously.

'Success?'

'Big success!' Kaine nodded. 'I'm so hungry.'

'Doesn't your mother cook for you?' said Mamma. 'What's wrong with her? Don't you worry. I'll speak to her. So, eat. A hungry man is an angry man.'

Kaine did as he was told, savouring each mouthful. While he was eating, he counted all of his grandmother's sprinting medals. From Combermere School all the way through to the National Track Finals, they charted her success during her days growing up in Barbados. Now they were all proudly displayed on her walls.

'How do you know me so well, Mamma?' he asked.

'Listen to me, young man,' she said, fixing him with her stare. 'I knew about you before you even existed. I told Sam she was having twins before the doctor did. It was quite a big deal. And, don't forget, they weren't even married at the time. I was there the day you were born.

'Out came Roxy. She had to be first, of course! There she was, causing a ruckus straightaway; crying, and punching out her little fists. She looked like an angel, but boy she made a noise. And her skin was so light; I couldn't believe she had come out of Samantha's body.

'And then out you came, half an hour later, just after midnight. I remember thinking to myself: *They're twins, but they're going to have different birthdays!* And your skin, it was as black as mine and Samantha's. I never knew twins could look so different!'

Kaine laughed. He had long since given up trying to convince people who didn't know him that, genetically at least, he was half-white.

'I knew you instantly, Kaine,' said his grandmother. 'You are me. So, don't be surprised that I know what it takes to get you to cut your hair! And sit up straight when you're eating – don't slouch around!'

Kaine loved his grandmother. She had had a really hard life – the hardest Kaine could imagine – but she was still the best company of anyone that he knew. He took another bite and shook his head at how delicious it was.

'I love being here and being with you, Mamma,' he said. 'But don't you feel like you spend more time with me than you do with Roxy?'

'Listen,' she said, grabbing his hand. 'I like spoiling you, Kaine. And don't worry about Roxy. She won't allow herself to lose out on too much of anything in life.'

'Run!' Roxy could hear her dad shouting as she hared around the court, chasing after the continuous stream of balls that he was blasting down.

Mr Kerrigan had allowed the two of them use of the Academy's tennis court before school on the strict understanding that they finished by 8.30 a.m. sharp and that Roxy was never late for lessons.

The balls were coming faster and faster now, her dad raining down shots for her to practise her groundstrokes.

'Take it earlier,' he shouted. 'Earlier! Before you can even smell the ball, you need to be into it.'

Roxy could feel her lungs, her heart and her brain all screaming for her to stop. There was a thumping ache in her head and a searing pain in her thigh, but she knew there were no breaks. The last time she had asked for one, her dad had made the session twice as long.

Now he seemed to be increasing the power even further, hammering the balls at her.

'Earlier! Are you listening to me, Roxy?'

Racing to her right, Roxy mistimed a forehand. The ball clipped the top edge of her racket and ricocheted up into her face. It went straight into her nose and stung painfully. She could feel drops of blood snake their way down her nostril. She sniffed them back up and swallowed them down.

While her dad was checking a new coaching session on his phone, Roxy scampered around the court's edges to collect the balls. Slowing down, she practised trying to walk how Jasmine and Tochi did at school. She allowed her hips to move more freely.

'Stop mucking around and come here now, Roxy!' said Daryll.

Mortified, Roxy immediately turned the walk into a sprint and headed to the net where he was waiting for her. Looking at the bristles of blondish brown hair on his shaved scalp, his thick, muscly body . . . there was no doubt where she got her skin colouring and physique from.

'Now, in the Finals on Sunday, Roxy,' he said, 'I want you to destroy every opponent you face. Whatever their weak spot is, you find it, you seek it out, and then you go in for the kill. OK?'

She nodded.

'Good,' Daryll continued. 'We know all the other players. The only one you have to worry about is Annabelle Taylor.'

Roxy grimaced. Annabelle Taylor was the player she

hated playing against more than any other. Not only did she have the infuriating habit of bouncing the ball way too many times before serving but, the last time they had faced each other in a tournament, at the change of ends, Annabelle had held her nose and asked Roxy when she had last taken a shower. It had put Roxy off, and after she had lost, her dad had refused to speak to her for two whole days.

'She's been training in America over Easter, working on her serving and volleying,' he said. 'So, if she's going to come to the net, what do we need to work on?'

'The lob,' Roxy said.

'Correct,' he said. 'Laced with topspin.'

Roxy watched as he reached into his bag to pull out two new tubes of balls. Immediately she felt the pressure pile further upon her. They had no money, and yet he was still spending on her tennis. What if she lost on Sunday? What would they do then?

She saw her dad's neck vein start to throb. One of the cans had already been opened and a new ball was missing. They both knew who was responsible.

Kaine bounced the brand-new tennis ball on the ground as he pushed open the classroom door and slumped down in the back row, taking his usual place in between AJ and Charlie McQueen. For a second, everyone turned and stared at him before re-focusing their attention on the whiteboard. Kaine Campbell being late was far from unusual, especially in recent months.

'Nice of you to join us, Kaine,' said Mr Hollis, a short, podgy, sweaty man with curly grey hair. 'Is there a reason that you're arriving half an hour after my lesson began?'

'Yeah,' said Kaine, refusing to make eye contact with the history teacher. 'I had something important I needed to do.'

'Well . . . would you like to share with us what it was that was so important to have kept you?'

'I was learning how to do a rabona, if you must know, sir,' said Kaine. 'I mean, realistically, in my life, that's going to be way more important than knowing how many wives Henry the Ninth had, isn't it?'

The rest of the class started laughing. There were even a few claps for the audacity of Kaine's response.

'Eighth,' said Mr Hollis.

'What?' said Kaine.

'Henry the Eighth,' said Mr Hollis. 'There was no

such person as Henry the Ninth, unless, of course, you're referring to Henry Benedict Stuart, who was known by the Jacobites as Henry the Ninth. Is that who you're talking about?'

'Erm, you've lost me, sir,' said Kaine. 'But this is my exact point: I can't do history but I can do football. Look. I'll show you.'

Kaine stood up and took the tennis ball out of his pocket. He pointed to the rubbish bin before dropping the ball to the ground. Then, twisting one foot behind the other, he stab-chipped the ball into the air with backspin. It looped straight into the rubbish bin first time.

The whole class burst into instantaneous cheers and applause, with Charlie McQueen leading a chant of: 'He's one of our own, he's one of our *owwwn*, Kaine Campbell, he's one of our own!'

'OK, that's enough, thank you!' Mr Hollis now said, trying to be heard above the cheers of Kaine's classmates. 'Lovely though your singing voices are, this is history, remember. Not music.'

'That's a rabona, sir,' said Kaine. 'And that's what I needed to perfect.'

'Very good,' said Mr Hollis. 'Even I can see that

takes some doing. How's all the football going, by the way? Are you signed up to a professional club?'

Kaine shrugged his shoulders.

'What was that?' Mr Hollis pressed.

'No,' murmured Kaine. He kicked the desk forward with such power that AJ and Queenie, who had been leaning on it, almost fell off their chairs. 'Just do your lesson!' he added, before muttering under his breath, 'stupid, boring man.'

While his teacher carried on talking, Kaine got out his headphones and started listening to some music. He knew Mr Hollis would pretend not to see.

Roxy watched all the other kids leave school and head down the road to the chicken shop. She wished she could go with them. She could almost taste that perfect breadcrumb coating. She shook her head and went into the toilets to put her tracksuit back on.

By the time she had come out, school was practically deserted. She sent a text to her mum before trudging towards the court.

Going to practise at school.
Dad's coming later.

'By the way, BIG news,' said AJ as he, Kaine and Charlie McQueen made the short walk to the chicken shop after school. 'Keep Saturday night free. My mum and stepdad might be going to Birmingham to visit my cousins. If they go, my brother says it's cool to have a party.'

'Sweet,' smiled Kaine. He and AJ would make full and proper use of a free house if it came off. The pair of them had been best friends since primary school and were, without doubt, the coolest boys in Year 9. They were always together and always had each other's backs.

'Am I invited, AJ?' Charlie asked.

A posh boy with extremely blond hair whose dream in life was to become Kaine and AJ's best friend, Charlie had started latching onto them a couple of months ago and managed to make himself a permanent fixture in their lives. If anyone else had tried to do that, Kaine wouldn't have stood for it but, somehow with Queenie, it seemed to be coming from a good place.

'Course you're invited,' said AJ, putting his arm around Charlie as they walked into the chicken shop. 'No party's complete without Queenie. Everyone knows that!'

'Yes!!' said Queenie, leaping into the air with excitement.

'Hey, my man Sami, sort me out with some chips, geez!' said Kaine to the shop owner, trying his usual trick of getting some food without having any actual money to pay for it.

'Hey, Kaine! How are you? And where is your sister? She never comes here any more!'

'Dad's banned her,' said Kaine. 'Just means there's more for me though. Come on, Sami, I'm starving!'

'How much you have?' asked Sami, as he lowered the fries into the sizzling oil. It was a hot afternoon and Sami was wearing a vest, which showed the dense, black hair on his arms, back and shoulders. Sami did not look like the most hygienic chef in the world. Today, there were even a couple of big, angry spots on his neck that looked just ready to be squeezed. Yet, despite this, his chicken shop remained the number-one destination for all the Compton kids after school.

'No money, man,' said Kaine. 'Sort me out though, Sam. Please, mate . . . I'll show you some skills!'

With the chips being nearly ready, this was Kaine's chance. He took the tennis ball out of his pocket and started balancing it on his forehead. Then he let it drop down to his foot and started keeping it in the air with all parts of his body.

Seeing what was happening, a group of the Compton kids came into the shop from the street to watch Kaine's skills. Queenie was filming everything on his phone, singing his 'One of our own' song, while AJ added to the atmosphere by beatboxing.

'You are an amazing player!!' shouted Sami, punching the air as Kaine finished his performance. 'Like an English Messi. I give *you* chips now, you give *me* signed shirt when you are professional!'

'Deal!' said Kaine. 'And some for my mates too please, Sami!'

'OK,' said Sami, smiling. 'But you tell your sister, I also want her racket when she wins Wimbledon!'

Kaine, AJ and Queenie scoffed down their portions of hot, greasy chips with such speed that they burnt the backs of their throats. They were so consumed by their food that none of them noticed the black BMW with tinted windows parked on the other side of the road.

'Tell me about Barbados again, Mamma,' said Kaine. 'What's it like?'

He looked at his grandmother and tried to imagine her there. She was in her sixties now, but she still looked young and beautiful, and she never tired of telling Kaine how all the men still found her attractive and how all the women her age were jealous of her.

He watched as she closed her eyes and leaned back against her cooker.

'The nicest, most generous people you'll ever meet . . . And the stars . . . oh, the stars . . . at night, they come out so bright it's like a sprinkling of magic in the sky. We had a saying, our family. Whatever you want from life, imagine it, send it out to the stars and the universe, and they will send it back to you and make it happen . . .

'And then the beaches. The softest, most golden sand . . . the most beautiful turquoise ocean. When the sun shimmers on it, it makes it look like there are gems right there on the water. You just want to hug it! Now you're going to ask me why on earth I wanted to come to the UK, right?' she said, grabbing Kaine's cheek and pinching really hard as she filled the room with her hearty laugh.

'Owww!' said Kaine, holding his cheek. 'It sounds like paradise.'

'Yes,' she said, 'but nowhere in this world is perfect. We had troubles too. I thought I'd got away from gangs when I came here . . .'

Her voice trailed off, and for a while neither of them said anything as, quietly, they both contemplated what had happened in her life since she came to the UK.

Kaine looked at his grandmother's National Sprint Gold Medal. 'And tell me about your running,' he said. 'What did it feel like?'

'I felt like I was riding the wind,' she said. 'There's no other way to describe it.'

A while ago, Kaine had found some old footage of the race on YouTube. It was the Women's 100-metre Sprint Final at the Barbados National Championships, and he loved to watch it with her. He put it on again now, and he and his grandmother both held his phone. It was probably about the fiftieth time they had watched it together, but it still gave Kaine goose bumps. He couldn't believe she had been the fastest woman in her whole country.

'Listen, Kaine,' she said suddenly, pausing the race. 'Your mum and dad have asked me to talk to you. They are worried in case the football dream doesn't happen for you. They say you'll be fourteen soon, that football's too much of a lottery. They want you to do better at school. They want you to be more like—'

'Don't tell me,' said Kaine. 'They want me to be more like Roxy.'

'You got it.'

'And what do you think, Mamma?'

'Roxy is a force of nature,' she said. 'She can handle whatever's thrown at her. I love that girl, and she's going to do something special with her life, I just know it . . . but even though you're twins, you need something different.'

'What do I need?'

'I think you need people to believe in you. To trust you.'

Kaine nodded.

'Let me tell you about what I see when I go to sleep,' Mamma said, putting the phone down and clasping Kaine's hand tightly. She had soothingly cool hands, and whenever Kaine could feel his body or his anger over-heating, just holding his grandmother's hand seemed to calm him down.

'Every night, when I close my eyes, the same picture comes into my head. It's you, sprinting on a football pitch, riding the wind, just like me. I send that image out to the stars, and I know it's going to come back to us.'

She held Kaine's hand even tighter now.

'You're going to be a star, Kaine,' she said. 'And don't let anyone tell you you're not. And that includes my daughter and my son-in-law. Do you understand me, Kaine? You can do things that other people can't. I'm not telling you that to big you up – I'm telling you that because it's true. You need to be aware of it. When there is a chance to do the normal, ordinary thing . . . you *don't* do that, Kaine. You do the special . . . you do the extraordinary. Because you are never ordinary, Kaine. You hear me?'

Kaine nodded.

'Never ordinary,' he repeated.

Kaine was waiting outside the chicken shop for AJ and Queenie who had gone back inside to scrounge some ice cream to soothe their burnt throats. He saw Mr Kerrigan walking up the street towards him and smiled.

Mr Kerrigan, who was Head of PE and the Deputy Principal, was a bit of a legend in school. He had played semi-professional football in Manchester when he was younger and he hadn't lost his touch; whenever he joined in during training, he was the only defender who could tackle Kaine. But it wasn't just because of the football that people respected Mr Kerrigan. It was the air of calm strength that he carried with him.

'Hey, legend,' said Kaine. 'What's happening?'

'I've got some news for you, Kaine Campbell,' Mr Kerrigan said. 'What would you say if I told you that a scout from Southampton might be coming to watch our match on Wednesday, to check you out?'

Kaine's heart started to soar. 'I'd say, are you for real?! Please tell me you're serious. Please don't tell me you're winding me up!'

'I'm deadly serious,' said Mr Kerrigan.

Kaine was bouncing up and down on the pavement. 'But . . . how . . . like . . . how did they hear about me?'

'Let's just say, I pulled a few strings,' said Mr

Kerrigan. 'You know I think you've got something. Well, now's the time to prove it.'

Kaine felt as though his whole body was being lifted into the air. This was the moment he dreamed of every night. The day that someone would give him a chance.

'And you realize this isn't just any old club, don't you, Kaine? There's a reason why it was Southampton that I got in touch with.'

'Course!' said Kaine. 'They brought through Bale, didn't they?' For a moment he allowed himself to imagine a career that would take him to all of Europe's greatest clubs, even to winning the Champions League with Real Madrid.

'That's right,' said Mr Kerrigan. 'And, going back, players like Le Tissier and Shearer too. They know how to produce players at Southampton all right. You know Shearer made his full debut when he was only seventeen. And you know what he did? He scored a hat trick. Away. Against Arsenal. Three years' time, Kaine. You reckon you could be doing that?'

'I'll have a bit of that,' said Kaine. 'Thank you so much, sir! You're such a legend!' He gave his teacher a huge and powerful hug.

However, their embrace was interrupted as a car

drew up right next to the kerb on which they were standing. One of the tinted windows of the black BMW was lowered to reveal a man, dressed in a suit, sitting in the back. The man was smoking a cigar and speaking on the phone, but he smiled and nodded at Kaine as the car smoothly eased away down the road.

Kaine watched him go by and held his breath. Sheldon Statham was the man who ran the Compton Estate. Nothing happened on the estate without his knowing about it or approving it. Lots of the boys worked for him, but this was the first time he had ever acknowledged Kaine. He felt both lucky and scared at the same time.

Kaine became aware that Mr Kerrigan was now fixing him with his stare.

'I've gone out on a limb to get this scout down for you, Kaine,' he said. 'But I need to know that you understand what an important time this is in your life.' He spoke very slowly, not taking his eyes off Kaine for a second. He had a wiry strength and his shaved head combined with his piercing blue eyes gave him the air of a warrior. 'And every little choice you make – from what you say . . . to how you act . . . to the *people* you decide to mix with – will have a far greater impact than you could ever imagine.'

'I won't let you down, sir. I promise you,' said Kaine, understanding who his teacher was referring to. 'My family . . . we stay away from people like Sheldon Statham . . . we always have . . . But, sir,' he said, quickly remembering his excitement about the scout. 'What happens if I do well? What happens if they like me?'

'I expect they'd want you to go down over the weekend and train with them, maybe play in a trial game. I think they play on Sundays.'

'Sunday? Oh my GOD!' said Kaine. 'I can't believe this is actually happening!'

'What's happening?' said AJ as he and Queenie finally emerged from the shop.

'A scout's coming to watch me play in the match on Wednesday!' said Kaine. 'This is it!' He high-fived his friends. 'I'll show them everything I've got, sir,' he said. 'The works!'

'Just remember what I said, Kaine,' Mr Kerrigan responded. 'Life is about choices. Make sure you make the right ones.'

Kaine nodded, but in truth, his brain had moved on from the warnings about Sheldon Statham. All he could think about was that this was the greatest day of his life.

It was a close, muggy evening and the atmosphere was heavy. After two hours at the tennis court practising by herself, Roxy's arms were leaden and her body was aching. Even though her dad hadn't turned up, she knew she couldn't leave in case he came later to check up on her. She tried another serve, but her timing was off. She caught the ball at the wrong angle and watched as it snapped hard into the tape of the net.

She sat down to take a break.

'What do you think you're doing? Stamina could be the key on Sunday.'

Roxy turned to see her dad, who must have snuck up behind her. He was filming her on his phone. He did it so he could go back later and show her what she had done wrong. It was one of things he had started doing in the last few months. She hated it.

'Hi,' she said. 'How did the interview go?'

As soon as she had asked the question, she knew she'd made a mistake.

'Show me some serves,' he said. 'Give me fifty.'

Roxy could feel the constant thudding in her head. He obviously hadn't got the job. 'I've already done two hundred,' she muttered. 'And I've got a really bad headache.'

'Stop talking and start serving!' ordered Daryll, still filming.

Roxy could smell the alcohol on his breath from where she was standing. It made her feel sick. She tossed the ball into the air and sent a thunderous serve straight down the middle. It was close to perfect.

'More snap in the wrist!' he barked. 'Do you still want to be number one in the world one day or not?'

When he got angry at her like this, Roxy wanted to shout back. She wanted to turn around and yell at her dad to shut up and back off. That this was *her* dream, not his. But one look at her dad's bloodshot eyes was enough to quell her inner rebellion. She tossed another ball into the air and raised her weary arm towards it.

Diary,

I have a confession to make. I cut Kaine's boots yesterday. I don't even know why I did it. I just feel like ~~I was~~ I'm stressed the whole time and he goes around doing whatever he wants, saying whatever he wants, and . . . I just want him to feel a bit of what I feel every day. Plus, he's so mean to me at school, so why can't I be mean back to him?

Dad's getting worse too. I know why he's doing it but it's not fair. Even when he's not there, I can still hear him, shouting at me, pushing me. He's taken all the ~~fun~~ joy away. I used to love the game so much. Now he's starting to make it feel like a prison.

It was 7p.m. when Kaine opened the front door and practically floated in through it. He was surprised to find his mum at home.

'Hi, Mum, how was work?' he said. She looked tired, and he could see a bead of sweat trickling down her forehead.

'Er, are you an alien? Have you abducted my son?' Samantha said. She was doing the ironing, but she stopped and moved towards Kaine. 'Work was fine, thank you for asking. Can I have a kiss while the going's good?'

Kaine laughed and managed to avoid her, grabbing a glass and filling it with cold water from the tap. Sammy's chips had made him so thirsty.

'Can't blame me for trying,' she said. 'Go on then, spill the beans. What's put you in such a good mood?'

'Oh, not much really,' he said, trying to keep the excitement from oozing out of every pore of his body. 'Just the small fact that, hopefully, I might be having a trial with Southampton Football Club this weekend!'

'Wow!' she said. 'Kaine, that's incredible!'

'I know! I've got a scout coming to watch me on Wednesday, and if it goes well, they'll want me to play in a match with them. Will one of you be able to take me down there?'

'I'm sure we can. When would it be?'

'Sunday.'

'I'm sure it'll be fine. I'm owed some time off from work. I'll do it.'

'Thanks, Mum,' said Kaine, giving her a quick hug, something he hadn't done for quite a while.

'My pleasure, Special K.' She smiled, folding one of his school shirts. 'As long as your dad doesn't need the car— Oh wait, hang on a minute. I'm being an idiot. We've got Roxy's County Finals on Sunday, haven't we?'

'How should I know?' said Kaine.

'Well, it's a pretty big deal, Kaine,' said his mum, shaking her head. 'It's what they've been training towards for months. Don't you even care any more?'

'Why is everything always about Roxy?' Kaine yelled. 'Forget it! I'll get a lift from someone who actually cares about *me*!' He chucked his glass into the sink and saw it smash.

'Come back here right now and clean up this mess!' Samantha shouted as he stomped off towards his bedroom.

Kaine ignored her, locking his door behind him.

9 p.m.

Diary,

Feeling a bit better now. At least I can say that some good stuff happened today, as well as the usual bad stuff. Will break down both sides for you.

BAD DAY: Tochi horrible as always at school. She saw my hair, came over, pretending to be all nice . . . said it looked really good . . . then she goes: 'Ah, did you do it yourself?' Hate her.

GOOD DAY: Heard AJ might be having a party on Saturday. I'm a 100% gonna go (even though it's the night before the Finals. I'll still find a way) but what I really want to see is how he invites me/what he says. I can't bear just being his friend (although he is the best friend anyone could ever have). Also, and I know this is so ~~cheez~~ cheesy, but I just love the way he smells. I don't know whether it's his deodorant or just natural but he just smells so much better than any other boy.

BAD DAY: Dad didn't get the job. Just means he's going to be even more on my case between now and Sunday. And that we still don't have any money.

GOOD DAY: Watched really closely how Jasmine flirts with the boys; the stuff she does with her hair, the way she tilts her head while she's talking to them. Reckon I can copy that. 😊

BAD DAY: I'd never have the guts to actually tell AJ how I feel.

GOOD DAY: For the first time in weeks, I didn't have a headache during the day at school. It only kicked in later. Mum says it's the 'changes' in my body (hate the way she says that word 'changes').

BAD DAY: Mum and Dad are shouting again now in the kitchen and the headache has come back twice as bad. Is my brain going to explode?

Kaine could feel the floor of his bedroom vibrating because of the disturbance that was coming from the kitchen next door. He took off his headphones and leaned against the wall to hear what they were arguing about this time.

'Are you joking me, Sam?' his dad was shouting. 'No chance. No way are me and Roxy taking the bus to the Finals. She needs the best possible preparation. Are you actually serious?'

'All I'm saying is . . . look, remember when we found out we were having twins? Remember what we said? We would always treat them equally.' His mum sounded upset.

'We *do* treat them equally, and *if* a scout comes to watch Kaine play on Wednesday that's great, but the fact is Roxy is *definitely* playing in the County Finals on Sunday, and we are not taking the bus there!'

'How about we wait to hear how Kaine does, and if he gets the trial we can discuss everything again then?'

'You're being ridiculous, Sam. We're talking about a trial that doesn't even exist yet. How do we know he's even telling the truth about the scout coming? It's typical Kaine. He knows how important Sunday is and he's just trying to cause trouble. Sometimes you have to make a decision and I'm deciding to use the car for Roxy on Sunday and that's it.'

'You say deciding, but all I can hear is choosing. You're choosing Roxy over Kaine. You know you are.'

Kaine heard a banging against the wall and a chair being kicked over.

'You can call it whatever you want,' Daryll shouted. 'But Roxy's got a real chance. She's *that close*. Do you understand what it could mean for this family? How it could change our lives? Football's a lottery. The amount of my mates that had trials. It never comes to anything. But tennis . . . we can actually do it. I know we can. If you trust me, I can make this thing happen. But we can't afford to start making changes and taking risks with our preparation now.'

'We can't afford much of anything at all, can we, Daryll?'

Kaine listened hard for his dad's response, but now he couldn't hear anything. It was when his dad went quiet that he was most threatening.

Kaine opened his bedroom door and picked up one of Roxy's old rackets, which was in the hallway. Then he moved into the kitchen and stood behind his dad who was towering over Samantha, pointing his finger at her.

'I'm trying my best for this family,' Daryll was saying. 'And we are on the verge of something special here. But if you keep questioning me and getting in the way, you're going to really wind me up . . .'

Kaine could hear the aggression in his dad's voice. Without thinking, he swung the racket at his dad's back, hitting him square between his broad shoulders. 'Leave her alone!' Kaine shouted.

Both shocked, his parents turned to face Kaine. His dad's face was bright red with rage. The vein in the side of his neck was pulsating.

For a second, there was silence.

Then Daryll laughed. It was a long, hoarse laugh that came right up from the bottom of his lungs. Kaine realized that the blow had not even hurt him.

'That's my boy,' he said, giving Kaine a painfully powerful slap on the back. Kaine could smell the alcohol on his dad's breath. 'Think you're the man of the house, eh? Think you're as big as me? Not quite yet, you're not. And if you think your mum's the one that needs protecting you should think again. She's stronger than the lot of us put together.

'That's my boy,' he repeated, slapping Kaine again, this time so hard he almost pushed him over. Kaine watched as his dad walked into the lounge and plonked himself down on the sofa, helping himself to another drink.

As he turned the TV on, he was shaking his head and still laughing to himself.

'And by the way,' he said, turning and smiling at Kaine. 'I'm using the car to take Roxy to the Finals on Sunday.'

TUESDAY

'What happened to you last night?' asked AJ, as Kaine sat down in between him and Queenie for French. It was the last lesson before lunch but the first one that they had together that day. 'I was messaging you all night, but you never replied.'

'Family rubbish,' said Kaine. 'Standard.'

The night had ended with his dad passed out in front of the blaring TV and his mum crying in their bedroom. Kaine had had to put his headphones on at top volume to drown out the sound as he tried to get to sleep. It hadn't worked.

'Right,' said AJ. 'Well, I've got something to cheer you up then. My mum and stepdad confirmed it. They *are* going to Birmingham Saturday, so that means—'

'Party?' said Kaine, not bothering to whisper.

'Serious party,' confirmed AJ. 'I texted everyone last night. They're all coming.'

'I knew it!' Queenie squealed, stretching out his arms and almost jumping into the air with delight. 'This will be my first proper one!!'

The rest of the class turned round, along with the teacher, Miss Claunt. 'What was that, Charlie? A party?' she said. 'Can everyone come?'

'I don't know, miss,' said Charlie. 'You'll have to ask AJ. It's at his . . . crib. His fam are going to Birm—'

'Yes, it's OK, Charlie,' interrupted Miss Claunt. 'We don't need all the details actually. What would be much better is if you could discuss the party in your own time and concentrate on your French while you're with me. Do you think you can do that?'

'*Oui*, miss,' said Charlie. '*Je suis très désolé.*'

Kaine and AJ were still laughing. They found everything Queenie did so funny. Especially his intense desire to be 'street'. 'Do I seem a *bit* "street" to you guys?' he'd often ask them. 'It's just, I do feel a *bit* street, you know, inside.'

'Of course, Queenie!' Kaine and AJ would say. 'OK,

we know your dad's an architect and your mum's an artist, but everyone can see you're a badman.'

The look of pride that would etch itself on Queenie's face only made the boys laugh even more. However, if anyone else at school laughed at Queenie or tried to mock him, they had Kaine and AJ to answer to.

'You got girls coming?' Kaine asked AJ as soon as Miss Claunt had once again turned her back.

'Yes, girls. Of course girls!' said AJ, fistbumping with Kaine. 'Ain't much of a party otherwise. No doubt.'

'Jasmine?'

'Already taken care of, bro. She's coming and she's bringing loads of her friends too.'

Kaine tried to not show his excitement too much. Jasmine had something. Or, rather, she had everything. Half-Vietnamese, half-black and so certain of herself, she made Kaine's brain sizzle.

'Will you make sure Roxy comes?' asked AJ.

'Shut up, AJ,' said Kaine, punching him under the table. 'I told you to drop it.'

'Ahh, come on, man,' said AJ, wincing at the power of Kaine's punch. 'I don't mean it in a bad way, I just mean, with all her tennis, can you make sure that she—'

'Just shut your mouth about my sister,' snapped

Kaine, leaning over and grabbing AJ by the shirt. 'Makes me feel sick.'

Once again, the class turned round, some smiling, some waiting to see what Kaine would do next. Looking like a child watching his parents argue, Queenie blurted out: 'It's OK, miss, they're just messing about. We're all best friends. The three of us. Like brothers. From other mothers. Come on, guys, take it easy, yeah?'

'Final warning,' said Miss Claunt. 'One more word from anyone and they'll be out.'

As order began to restore itself, Kaine watched Miss Claunt writing a series of words on the whiteboard. He had no idea what any of them meant and he did not care either. The only thing that mattered was that there were now only twenty-four hours until he would be playing in a school match and being watched by a top scout.

There goes Kaine Campbell, he wanted people to say when they saw him at school. *He's already been signed up, you know?*

Soon his real life would begin. Soon people would start to give him the respect he deserved.

His phone vibrated in his pocket. 'Yo!' said Kaine, answering the call immediately and making no attempt to hide it. It was one of the older boys from the estate.

'Yeah, I'm at school, but it's cool,' he said, stretching his feet out onto the desk. 'Not feeling this whole "school thing" at the moment anyway. Doing French – don't even know why I'm here. Never gonna have to speak French unless PSG sign me and I gotta go live in Paris.'

'Kaine Campbell! Turn that phone off and give it to me right now!' Miss Claunt shouted, her face contorting with anger.

'Shhh!' said Kaine, putting his finger to his lips. 'Can't you see I'm on a phone call, miss?' He sucked his teeth and shook his head.

'Out!' shouted Miss Claunt, storming over and grabbing the phone from Kaine's hands. 'Get out of my classroom and go and see Mrs Buckland *right now*!'

'**D**o you know why you're here, Kaine?' Mrs Buckland, the Principal of Compton Academy, asked him.

He knew why he was there all right. But that didn't mean he was going to answer her question.

'Are you even listening to me?' she was saying. 'What part of you thinks it's acceptable to conduct a phone call in the middle of a French lesson?'

Kaine just shrugged his shoulders. He and Mrs Buckland had fought this battle many times over the last few months. He looked at the photos on her desk. Her and her perfect family. He knew she lived in a nice house. He knew her husband had a good job and he'd seen them driving around on weekends in their Mercedes. He wasn't scared of her.

'Is that your daughter, miss?' he said, picking up one of the photos. 'She's well fit!'

'I have to ask you a serious question, Kaine,' the Principal said, taking the photo out of his hand. 'Why are you behaving like this? This isn't you. I know it's not. Where do you think this is all going? . . . What is it you want from your life, Kaine?'

'Be a footballer,' said Kaine, smiling at the prospect. His plan was pretty simple. He wondered why so many people had a problem understanding it.

'And you think any football club is going to want someone on their books who shows such a lack of respect for those around them?'

'Miss, football clubs want you if you can score goals. Simple. And scoring goals is what I do in my sleep. Ask Mr Kerrigan. I've even got a scout coming to watch me tomorrow.'

'You're wrong,' said Mrs Buckland in a firm voice. 'I've had pupils at other schools who have been signed up by academies. These clubs want to know everything that's happening at school. If I told a club the trouble you've been causing, they would fling you out faster than you can believe.'

Kaine shook his head and sucked his teeth. In truth, he actually thought Mrs Buckland was OK. He liked that her family originally came from St Lucia, a neighbouring island to Barbados, but the fact was they were on different sides. She wanted Kaine to behave at school and Kaine had had enough of behaving. He didn't see the point any more.

'Look,' she said in a warmer voice, taking off her glasses. 'I know what talent you and your sister have got. Anyone who makes Mr Kerrigan wax lyrical the way that he does about your football must be pretty special. I want to encourage and support you, Kaine. This school is right behind anyone who has a passion and a drive. And I know what your family has been through. I grew up with your uncle, don't forget that. But I cannot and will not stand by and let my staff be insulted and undermined. And if I need to use your football to control your behaviour then, believe me, I will have absolutely no hesitation in doing so. Do I make myself clear?'

'Can I go now?' said Kaine, standing up. He could see Jasmine was outside and he wanted to talk to her.

She nodded. 'Do not try to take me on,' she said. She had put her glasses back on and was writing something down. 'You don't know me, Kaine Campbell. But believe me, you will. Here – you can take this now.'

She handed Kaine his weekly report. Kaine took it and quickly shoved it into his bag without bothering to look at it.

'Hey, what happened, K-bomb?' asked Charlie McQueen, seemingly popping up out of nowhere as soon as Kaine left Mrs Buckland's office. 'Are you in trouble?'

'Nah, man,' said Kaine. 'She can't do nothing to me.'

He strutted down the hallway, whistling as he went, looking to see where Jasmine had gone.

However, somewhere in the back of his mind the sound of alarm bells started to ring.

It was lunch time, and Roxy sat down on a bench by the side of the playground and stared at AJ, who was talking to Jasmine and Tochi. Even though they weren't friends any more, Roxy still missed Jasmine. But she hated Tochi's guts. She was sure that it was Tochi who had told Jasmine to stop liking any of Roxy's photos online. It had started when they had come back for school last September, and no one had told Roxy why.

AJ and Jasmine and Tochi were probably all talking about his party. It sounded like the whole year was going, but she was still waiting for him to ask her.

She took out her phone to pretend she was doing her own thing. Checking her accounts, she saw she had lost even more followers. It was as though some secret message had been passed around to make it seem as though she was the most unpopular person in the whole school.

'Hey, Roxana, what's cooking?'

Roxy looked up to see that AJ had come over and sat down right next to her, and she immediately saw that Jasmine and Tochi were giving her evil looks from across the playground. *Fifteen–love*, she smiled to herself.

'Ah, nothing much, Alonso,' said Roxy, sitting on

her hands so he couldn't see how rough and calloused they were from all the tennis. She really liked the fact that AJ was the only person who called her by her full name. He had even told her what it meant, that it was a historic Persian name and it meant 'bright light'.

'So, listen . . .' smiled AJ.

While he was talking, Roxy closed her eyes for just the quickest of moments so she could smell him a bit better. She was sure he was about to ask her to the party.

'AJ!' shouted Kaine, who had suddenly appeared and was now talking to the girls. 'Jasmine and Tochi have both got temporary tattoos done on their necks – come and have a look!'

The girls were lifting up their hair to show Kaine, and they were now waving AJ over too. He stood up, giving Roxy a regretful smile. Roxy grimaced as she watched him walk over to the girls. *Fifteen–all.*

Kaine crept up behind Mamma and, without her knowing, started filming her on his phone while she was singing.

'*Don't look at me now, don't tell me those sacred lies, Don't look at me now, don't give me those big brown eyes . . .*'

It was Mamma's favourite song, and although it was an old one, Kaine loved it too. He had even downloaded it. He smiled as he filmed her belting it out while she was doing the washing-up. Meanwhile, in his own mind, he tried to work out why it was that whenever he was with her, he always felt happy.

'Mamma,' he said, putting down his phone. 'How come you never tell me what to do?'

Mamma shook her head. 'Now why would I want to tell you what to do?' she asked.

'Everyone else does.'

'Well, I'm not like everyone else, am I?' she said, starting to dance while she put the plates away. 'People just need to chill out! Life's too short.'

Kaine grinned. Sometimes his grandmother spoke like a teenager.

'You . . .' she continued, squeezing his cheek like she wanted to eat it. 'You look like me and your mum, but you've got your dad's temper. Boy, have you got his temper. Don't be riling up, Kaine Campbell,' she said, shaking her head. 'You might be biting off more than you know what to do with.'

She danced a few more steps and then handed Kaine her big casserole bowl to dry.

'You know what I used to say about you when you were younger?' she said. 'I used to call you my little lion cub. I knew you'd grow up to be a big, strong man and now you're nearly there. The women in our family. We know. We might be mad and crazy at times. But we know.

'Eh! Look me in the eye when I'm talking to you. And stand up straight! Show me how tall you're going to be.'

Kaine stood up as tall as he could, straightening his back and stretching his neck.

'See,' she said. 'Soon you'll be a lion. You'll have so much power in you . . . At first, you won't know what to do with it or how to control it . . . The day that you learn how to master that power is the day that you'll be a leader. Then you'll use your strength to help people when you don't have to. That's what real leadership is . . . But that's your journey, Kaine . . . No one can tell you how to get there.'

Kaine let her words sink in. He liked them.

'Let's have another song, Mamma,' he said, picking his phone up again to carry on filming.

'Eh, get that thing out of my face,' she said.

'Come on, Mamma, I'm just asking for one more song,' he said. 'You've been singing all day!'

Mamma looked into the camera and, with a glint in her eye, said: 'Now, go on. You know Mamma can't sing.'

Kaine shook his head. He wasn't the only one in the family who didn't like being told what to do!

'Finally!' said Roxy as Kaine arrived home that evening. 'You realize we all waited for you to have dinner and now it's eight thirty. I'm supposed to finish dinner by seven thirty! Where have you been?'

'Disneyland,' snapped Kaine, stomping through the hallway, giving Roxy the dirtiest of looks.

'What's for dinner?' he shouted over his shoulder.

'We're eating now,' said Daryll, standing up and walking towards Kaine, before physically hauling him down into a chair at the table. 'But first of all we need to hear your report. Roxy's read us hers. Now let's hear yours.'

'Haven't got it,' said Kaine.

'Liar,' said Roxy.

'Shut up, you scum!' said Kaine.

'Don't you dare speak to your sister like that,' said Daryll, grabbing Kaine's rucksack and pulling it off his back. 'We all know that Mrs Buckland wants us to go through these reports together.'

He emptied the contents of Kaine's bag onto the kitchen table. Chewing gum, broken pencils, old football magazines, loose change, headphones, two half-eaten chocolate bars, an empty packet of crisps and, finally, a very crumpled weekly school report all fell out.

'Told you,' said Roxy.

Kaine stood up and launched himself at Roxy, who only just managed to evade his clawing arms.

'Roxy, that's enough!' screamed her mum, her voice breaking as she shouted. 'You can take your dinner to your room. Your dad and me need to talk to Kaine.'

Roxy collected her bowl and went into her room. Then, after a couple of minutes, when she calculated that the coast would be clear, she quietly opened her bedroom door and tiptoed into Kaine's room. She could hear what was going on better from there. She leaned her ear against the wall and listened to Kaine reading out his report.

'Extra note from Mrs Buckland,' Kaine was saying, in his most bored voice. *'It seems the only thing that he cares about is football, so I have decided that if Kaine does not make fifty per cent or higher in his French test tomorrow morning, he will be suspended from the school football team with immediate effec—*

'What?!' said Kaine, breaking off from reading the report. 'She never said that to me! I'm playing in the match tomorrow. I've got to. I don't care what she says.'

There was a moment of silence, in which Roxy could imagine Kaine chucking the report onto the kitchen table. Then Roxy heard her mum continue reading Mrs Buckland's words.

'If this latest punishment does not work, I will be inviting you to my office to discuss excluding Kaine from this school. This is not what I want, but I'm afraid we have come to the end of the line. We need to see some effort and willingness from him in order to continue . . .

'Oh, Kaine,' Roxy heard her mum say. 'Is this really what you want? Do you really want to get yourself chucked out of school?'

'Don't care,' said Kaine.

'You really are the most stupid boy I've ever met in my life,' said Daryll.

'You can talk!' Kaine shouted back.

Roxy was desperate to see what was happening but scared at the same time. Kaine and her dad were both big. If they really went at each other, all hell could break loose.

'Come here,' she heard her dad growl.

'Daryll! Stop!' shouted Samantha. 'Leave him!'

The next thing Roxy heard was the front door slamming and the sound of Kaine sprinting down the steps.

Kaine was by the garages at the end of the estate, kicking stones against the garage doors. When he and Roxy were younger, they had spent thousands of hours here together; him kicking a football against the wall, her doing the same with a tennis racket and ball. All their old graffiti was still visible on the walls.

It was still one of the places he went to for escape. Although half an hour had passed since the argument about his report, he was still burning with anger. When he looked up and saw Roxy approaching, he shook his head.

'Can you just leave me alone?' he said, wiping away a tear before she could see it.

'Believe me, I don't want to be here,' Roxy said coldly, 'but Mum said to show you this.' She thrust an old photo into his hand. It was the four members of their family on the twins' seventh birthday. They were all standing in the park on a sunny day, and Kaine and Roxy were doing a high-five. When they were younger, when they got on, high-fives had been their thing. They always seemed to be able to get perfect timing. 'She told me to remind you that we're supposed to be a team.'

Kaine looked at Roxy standing angrily in front of him with her hands on her hips. Then he looked at the photo. It was only seven years ago, but it felt like a different lifetime. For a second, a memory of what it felt like to be that close to Roxy and his parents flickered into Kaine's mind, but he extinguished it immediately.

'You know you're going to make them get divorced if you carry on like this,' Roxy said. 'You should think about that. What you're doing to them. We know you blame us for what happened to Mamma. For not answering our phones. But it wasn't our fault. How could we have known? And don't think you're the only one in pain either. I still think about her every day too, you know.'

'Yeah,' said Kaine. 'You all cared so much you couldn't even be bothered to answer my calls. Do you know how many times I called you? All of you!'

He kicked a small rock against a garage door so hard that the pigeons that were sitting on the roof all hurriedly flew into the air, their wings flapping loudly as they went.

'Why are you always trying to wind me up?' he said. 'Like with that report. Tell me, I need to know. You're clearly their favourite anyway, so I don't get it. Why do you still need to wind me up and put me down the whole time?'

'I'm the favourite?!' said Roxy. 'Congratulations, Kaine – that's probably the most stupid thing you've ever said. Anyway, I'm not here to talk to you and I know that you don't want to talk to me either. I just came cos Mum asked me to give you the pho—'

'This?' said Kaine, tossing the photo into one of the nearby rubbish bins as he walked away. 'Why don't you go back and tell her that that family doesn't exist any more.'

Tuesday June 5

Diary,

It's 10 p.m. I'm really tired and I've got another headache but I need to tell you something. Because I need to say this. Get it out of my system.

My brother really is the most STUPID and ANNOYING boy on the planet and he actually has no idea about anything.

He's just said to me – again – that I'm Mum and Dad's favourite! I mean, how can he say that?!

URGGGGHHH! Can you imagine what would happen if I did the stuff he does? These days Dad literally controls my whole life. He watches every single thing I do, where I go, what I eat, who I talk to. I can't even go to the toilet without him knowing. I literally live in a prison. I can't do ANYTHING!!

And then Kaine acts like a complete ******** at school AND at home . . . and he gets away with all of it!

He thinks I'm their favourite. He has no idea!!

What if I told him that, at the moment, I don't even like tennis. That sometimes I even hate it . . . and yet it's my whole life. That means I actually hate my whole life. Shall I tell Kaine? If I told him the truth, what would he say then?

I can't believe he's the same boy who used to be my best friend. I can't believe he's the same person that I used to share my dreams with. We used to promise each other we would both make it right to the top one day and that we would support ~~both~~ each other all the way. We even used to say that we'd try not to have matches on the same day so that we could give each other all our strength for the other one to use. Can you believe that?! Can you believe that was how close we were? And now . . . now he's just an idiot who thinks he's being badly treated and I'm the enemy.

He should try just ONE DAY in MY LIFE.

Trust me, he wouldn't want to be in these shoes.

It was 10.15 p.m. and Kaine had been walking around the estate and the local streets for ages. It was a hot, humid night. He was sweating, starving and tired, but he refused to go home. He wished he never had to go back to that place.

He decided to stay out as long as he could, and even though he had no money, his plan was to go to all the takeaways – starting with Sami's – and try to scrounge something to eat when they closed. Then, when everyone was asleep, he'd go back. It was only really his boots that he was going back for. Otherwise, he would just as happily sleep on a bench in the park. But he needed those boots. The match was tomorrow. If he could get the Southampton scout to like him, to want to sign him, everything would change in an instant. It would be his ticket to another world.

Kaine's train of thought was interrupted by the sudden realization that he was being followed by a car. He could hear the purring sound of an engine right behind him. He turned round to see a gleaming black BMW right next to him in the road.

The tinted window slid down and Sheldon Statham beckoned Kaine towards him. 'Get in,' he said.

Kaine knew how dangerous it was to get into any

stranger's car, especially this one. He paused and looked down to the ground. All he could see was his old, busted trainers.

He opened the door and got in. The car felt like a cool desert of calm.

'I want to talk to you,' said Sheldon. 'Tidy yourself up.' He reached into his pocket and offered Kaine a packet of fresh wet wipes.

Kaine looked dubiously at the packet.

'Go on,' said Sheldon.

Kaine grabbed the packet and used three of the wipes to cool and clean his forehead and his neck. Then he scrunched them up and was just about to throw them out of the window when Sheldon grabbed his hand firmly.

'Don't do that,' he said. 'Marcel will take that for you.'

With that, the driver wordlessly reached his gloved hand behind him to take the wet, grimy wipes from Kaine and place them in a small plastic container between the front seats.

Kaine noticed there wasn't a hair out of place on Sheldon Statham's head. Nor was there a speck of dust on his clothes or an inch of fat on his body. Even though he had run the Compton Estate for years, he still looked quite young and fit, and Kaine suspected that in a fight, Sheldon would still be lightning quick.

'So, Kaine, you're a footballer, are you?' asked Sheldon.

'How d'you know that?' Kaine shifted back in his seat. He felt another trickle of cold sweat drip down his back. He had never told Sheldon his name.

'Are you fast?' enquired Sheldon.

'No one quicker than me,' said Kaine.

'Are you strong?'

Kaine pulled up his sleeve and flexed his bicep.

Sheldon nodded. Then he took out a cigar, lit it, and took a long drag. Kaine could feel the intense weight of Sheldon's stare.

'You've got attitude, haven't you?' Sheldon said. 'But, tell me, what scares you?'

'Nothing,' said Kaine.

'Drop the act,' said Sheldon. 'You can be honest with me.'

'Only thing that scares me,' said Kaine, 'is being stuck in this place. I'm gonna do something with my life. Be someone. People gonna know my name. I'm gonna be one of the best players in the world.'

'From a little spark may burst a flame,' said Sheldon.

'What?' said Kaine.

'Now,' said Sheldon, taking another long drag of his cigar and looking at the time on his gold watch, 'let's get you some food.'

'Mamma, can I ask you something,' said Kaine. They were watching a quiz show together after school. Mamma was sitting down drinking tea while Kaine was standing up, practising kick-ups with a ping-pong ball.

'You know you can ask me anything,' she replied, squeezing his cheek as he sat down next to her.

'How come Mum doesn't ever talk about what happened to Uncle Anthony? She talks about what an amazing brother he was and how much he would have loved us all, but she doesn't talk about . . . you know . . .'

Kaine could see Mamma's body tense as he raised the subject. She slowly put down her cup of tea and turned off the TV. For a long while she was silent. Then she turned to look at Kaine. He could feel her staring deep into his eyes, searching for some kind of answer.

'When your mum was growing up, we talked about your uncle Anthony every day,' she said finally. 'It was the right thing to do. We wanted it to be OK to grieve and we wanted to keep the blessing of his life alive. But, you're right, after a while, though we still talked about him – as a person – always, we started to talk about . . . what happened less.

'You're his age now . . . the age he was . . .' she said,

looking at him tenderly. 'So I think maybe we should talk about it.'

'Before I show you this, Kaine,' said Mamma, pointing to a locked black box that she had brought down from upstairs, 'I want to tell you a bit more of my story. Is that OK?'

Kaine nodded.

'So, I was national track champion,' she began. 'You know that. I was heading for the Olympics, and I was also one of the most beautiful girls on the island. I don't say that to boast. It is just a fact. I was eighteen and I loved my boyfriend very much. His name was John and he was ten years older than me. He was my coach.

'John got offered a job to work with the British athletes and he wanted to take it. He wanted me to go with him, and I wanted that desperately too. To make my father happy, we got married, then we came to England, and within six months, I was pregnant.

'For a long while, I thought everything was perfect. Anthony was born and then, six years later, Samantha joined us. But within three months of Sam being born, John told me he had fallen in love with another woman

– one of his British runners – and that he was leaving to start another family with her.

'I still remember it like yesterday. As he walked out of the door, I pulled Anthony and Samantha into my arms, gave them a huge hug and told them that we didn't need anyone else. Everything was going to be OK. And I made sure it was. I must have had about six different jobs: cleaning, typing, sewing . . . I didn't think about the sprint champion I could have been in another universe. I had my children. They were my medals. They were my achievement.

'We ate a hot dinner together every night with a smile on our face, and that was all I craved and cared about. And the kids, they turned out good. Better than good. And what made me happier than anything was how they loved each other.

'As he got older, I knew I could rely on Anthony more to look after and protect Sam. It was a tough area and he knew it was his job to help me keep us all safe. Never once did he get in trouble with the police. Never once did he cause any problems. He simply had the kindest smile you will ever see. And he was so clever that the school told me, if he kept working hard, he would be able to go to university. The first in our family. My Anthony.

'I still remember waving them off that morning. He

was taking Sam to her school before going on to his own . . . And then, that afternoon, it happened.'

Mamma took out a key, unlocked the box and pulled out a collection of old newspaper cuttings from inside.

She handed one to Kaine.

BOY, 14, STABBED TO DEATH

Model student, Anthony Augustine, killed in what is believed to be a case of mistaken identity as he waited to pick his sister up after school. Tragedy linked to gang battles on the notorious Compton Estate (continued on next page)

Kaine looked at his grandmother. He had no words.

'I was in a local shop, picking up some groceries for dinner when I heard the sirens,' said Mamma. 'I knew. I just knew. I dropped the bags and ran out of the shop towards Sam's school. I ran through the crowd, pushing my way to the front, and there he was, lying there, surrounded by blood. So much blood. I picked up his head and stroked him and told him to wait. That it would just be a minute. Help was already here. He tried to smile. That beautiful smile. He could barely speak, but he still whispered: "I love you, Mum."'

Kaine saw a tear drop from Mamma's eyes and he started crying too. He went to hug her and they held onto each other.

'I'm sorry, Kaine,' she said. 'I know it's difficult, but it's important you hear this.'

Kaine nodded.

'But . . . why did they do it?' asked Kaine.

'Same as always,' said Mamma. 'Territory, control, money . . . knives . . . So many beautiful young men dead because of knives . . . And it never stops. Once the first drop of blood is shed, soon enough it becomes a river . . . I kept the kids away from it as much as I could. But that day it came to us. It was one gang trying to warn another to stay off their patch. They just got the wrong boy. Anthony was the wrong person, in the wrong place, at the wrong time. They stabbed him in the back, and he had lost too much blood. The stains were there on the pavement for weeks afterwards. He died just before we reached the hospital. And, Kaine, your mum . . . little Samantha . . . she had been the first one out of school . . . and she saw the whole thing.'

Kaine closed his eyes. 'But . . .' he said. 'Who . . . ?'

Mamma shook her head and looked at her hands, which had ink stains on them from all the old newspaper cuttings.

'Samantha was the only person who saw it, but she was too young . . . much too young . . . We never found out who.'

It was midnight by the time Kaine eased the door of the flat open.

As predicted, his dad was asleep on the sofa, and he crept quietly to his room so as not to have to endure an interrogation from his mum or his sister.

He picked up his boots and placed them next to his bed. Then he got under his duvet and replayed the night's events in his head.

Sheldon had told Marcel to drive over to Dante's, the posh Italian restaurant in town.

'Marcel, take Kaine in and get him an escalope Milanese, will you please?' Sheldon had said when they had arrived. 'I'll stay in the car. I have some calls to make.'

'What's an esco milan-thing?' Kaine had questioned.

'Esc-al-ope Mil-an-es-e,' Sheldon had repeated, carefully pronouncing each syllable. 'Breaded veal with fresh pasta in a tomato sauce. Trust me,' he had said smoothly, resting his hand reassuringly on Kaine's shoulder. 'I own the restaurant. It's good.'

Kaine had accepted the advice and gone inside the restaurant with Marcel, who was greeted like a friend by all the waiters. Fifteen minutes later, having wolfed down the entire meal, Kaine was already getting back into the BMW.

Sheldon was on the phone. 'Yes, I'll deal with it,' he was saying. 'For good.'

When he finished his call, he paused for a moment and then turned to Kaine.

'Well, you did say you were fast. How was the meal?'

'First time I've been in a place like that.' Kaine beamed. 'And the waiters told me the meal I had comes from Milan. AC Milan is my favourite team in Serie A!'

'Good,' said Sheldon. 'Now, take this.' He took out a large, clipped bundle of money. He pulled out a note and handed it to Kaine. It was a fifty. Kaine looked at it, but did not move. 'Go on,' said Sheldon, folding Kaine's hand around it. 'Buy some new shoes.'

Kaine looked down again at the pieces of rubbish that he was wearing. He stuffed the money into his sock.

'I want you to join my team, Kaine,' said Sheldon.

'What do you mean, "join your team"?' said Kaine. He could feel his blood going cold. Mr Kerrigan's warnings were echoing in his mind, but he could also feel the fifty-pound note nestling nicely in his sock.

'I like you. I want you to do some little jobs for me, and in return, I'll pay you and make sure you are safe. Here,' he said. 'You'll need this.' Sheldon reached into his jacket pocket and slid what looked like a credit card across to Kaine.

'What is it?' said Kaine.

'All it needs is three folds,' said Sheldon taking it back. 'You release the catch, flip the blade out and then fold the flaps into a handle.' Sheldon was now holding a pocketknife. It was razor sharp. 'Go on,' he said. 'Have a look.'

Kaine took the knife in his right-hand. It was shockingly light and devastatingly sharp. He stared at its point.

'It's yours,' said Sheldon.

Kaine felt himself shiver. 'Thanks,' he said. 'But I don't want it. My family . . . we . . . I'm not interested in knives.' He handed the knife back.

'That's all well and good,' said Sheldon. 'But what are you going to do if someone comes at you . . . ? These are dangerous streets. You need to protect yourself, Kaine.'

Kaine thought about Rufus Blackstock from the estate. He remembered the throat-slitting gesture Rufus had made on Sunday night. He wondered what he would do if Rufus came at him with his knife. For a moment he wavered . . . 'Sorry,' he said, regaining himself. 'Like

I told you, it's a family thing. We're against knives . . . You better take this back too because I'm not going to work for you. I'm all about football. That's it. That's everything.'

Kaine took the money out from his sock. Statham smiled and considered Kaine, looking him up and down.

'You can keep it,' he said finally. 'And this is what we're going to do: I'll give you my number, and when you change your mind, you'll call and we'll have another conversation.'

'Fine,' said Kaine. 'But I won't change my mind.'

'We'll see,' said Sheldon. 'You'll remember tonight, Kaine . . . it's the beginning of always.'

Kaine had shrugged his shoulders, got out of the car and headed home. But although he was sure he'd made the right decision in rejecting the knife, he wasn't able to shake off the feeling that, one day, he and Sheldon Statham would meet again.

WEDNESDAY

It was break time, and Kaine and AJ were heading to the canteen to get something to eat.

'Wagwan, mandem!' said Charlie McQueen popping up out of nowhere, following in their wake.

Kaine and AJ each gave him a fistbump. 'All good, Queenie, all good!' Kaine replied. 'I can't be doing with this queue, though. I need to get food quick cos I want to have a kickaround in break to warm up for the match later.'

Kaine was flying. He'd woken up still tasting his high-class restaurant meal and had hidden his newly acquired fifty-pound note in his sock drawer. Walking to school that morning, he had felt untouchable. Not only was he about to put his skills on show for a professional club scout, but he had also turned down Sheldon Statham. No one turned down Sheldon Statham! Apart from Kaine Campbell.

Looking at the length of the queue, he knew there would be no time for football if he hung around waiting to reach the front. Spotting Roxy, who was just about to be served, he gestured for AJ and Queenie to follow him.

'Thanks for saving my place,' he said, barging in front of her.

'Oi!' shouted Roxy. 'Get to the back! I've been here for ten minutes!'

'Shut up, Roxy!' said Kaine. 'I'm doing you a favour – more food's only gonna make your thighs even bigger.'

'Kaine, man!' said AJ. 'That's out of order!'

Roxy left the queue and ran outside.

'What?' said Kaine, pointing after her. 'It was only a joke, for God's sake! And now look at how she's overreacting! This is what I have to put up with.'

He ordered and ate his sandwich in the space of a minute and then went to join his regular game of break-time football.

'You ready for the French test?' asked Queenie, who

had been watching Kaine play, as they made their way back inside.

'Yes,' said Kaine. 'I've been thinking about this French test quite a lot actually. Buckland said I have to get fifty per cent otherwise I'm banned from playing for the school team.'

'What?!' said Queenie. 'But what if you don't get it? Isn't the scout coming this afternoon?'

'Yup,' said Kaine.

'That's harsh,' said Queenie. 'What are you going to do?'

'I'm gonna do what I have to,' said Kaine, smiling. 'See you later, Queenie.' He winked at him and made his way down the corridor. The idea had come to him just as he'd arrived at school this morning, and he knew it was genius the moment he thought of it.

Standing in front of the fire alarm, as casually as he could in the midst of the end-of-break-time rush, Kaine gathered together all the power his body contained. Then he wrapped his tie round his hand and clenched it into a fist.

Roxy found a bench away from everyone. She didn't want them to be able to see the tears in her eyes. She hated herself for being so fragile. How could just a few cruel words from Kaine kill her from the inside? She should be immune to it now, the amount of times he'd done it, especially in the last few months, but it still hurt just as much each time.

She took out her phone and started scrolling through everyone's photos, comparing all the other girls' thighs to her own. She saw Tochi had unfollowed her now too. She unfollowed Tochi straightaway in response.

'There you are,' said AJ, coming to sit down next to her. 'I've been looking for you.'

Roxy wiped her eyes and turned away.

'He shouldn't have said that,' said AJ. 'It was out of order. I'll speak to him.'

'Good luck,' said Roxy. 'Anyway, he's right. My body is disgusting. All these muscles. I look like a man.'

'You've got an incredible body,' said AJ.

Roxy caught her breath as he looked directly at her.

'Why are you so hard on yourself? You look amazing, and what you do is incredible. You're the best tennis player I've ever seen.'

Roxy shook her head. 'What if I told you that . . . I don't even like tennis at the moment? What if I told you I hated it?'

She was surprised to hear the words come out of her mouth. AJ was the first person she had told how she was feeling.

'You don't mean that. You're going to be one of the best players in the world,' he said. 'Everyone can see it.'

'I do mean it.'

'OK, so why do you play then? You don't have to.'

'You don't understand. I do have to.'

'Why?'

'It's my dad . . . you know he lost his job, don't you?'

'Yeah, Kaine said.'

'That's when it changed. In the last few months, it's like he thinks my tennis is his new job. Because we can't afford private coaching any more, he's decided he's my coach, and he won't leave me alone for one second. He's suffocating me, and I can't bear it. All the love I had for tennis. It's gone. He's taken it away.'

'So just tell him. Tell him to back off.'

'Have you seen my dad?' said Roxy. 'He's not the kind of guy you tell what to do. And anyway, it's not like I don't want to win. I do. I want it more than anything.

I just want it to be mine . . . and it feels like he's stolen it from me.'

'That's tough,' said AJ.

'I don't know how you do it, AJ,' she said. 'But somehow you make me feel like it's OK to talk to you. To tell you all my rubbish.'

'It's not rubbish. It's your feelings,' said AJ. 'Look, Roxana, all I know is that you're an amazing person and . . . I just know you'll find a way. You always do.'

Roxy wanted to hug him with all her might. 'Thanks for not judging me,' she said, feeling herself start to blush again. 'You're . . . special.'

'Friends don't judge each other,' he said, leaning into her and softly touching his shoulder onto hers. 'We're friends, right?'

Roxy could feel her whole body deflate. 'Yeah,' she said. 'Friends.'

She looked at the ground and, with another crushing blow, realized that he still hadn't even invited her to his party. She was just about to raise it with him when the deafening sound of the alarm bell came ringing out from the main school building.

'Let me be absolutely clear,' Mrs Buckland was saying to the 1,200 pupils of Compton Academy who were standing in rows on the school playground. 'There was no fire, but this was no fire drill. It was a blatant act of vandalism by someone, which is going to lead to an entire period of the day being lost for every student in this school. Whoever you are, we will find you, and you will be punished. Severely.'

Roxy was fuming. Not because the fire alarm had been set off but because of when. She had been *that* close to asking AJ about the party. She surreptitiously stole a look at him now as he stood in the row next to her. Somehow he even managed to have a cool way of standing still. Then Roxy saw Kaine, who was next to AJ. She detected the thinnest outline of a smirk on Kaine's face. Instantly, she knew who had set off the alarm.

'How you feeling, main man?' said Mr Kerrigan. Kaine looked up from tying his laces and smiled. It was 2.30 p.m., the match was about to begin and, most importantly, he was free to play. His plan had worked to perfection. The entire period after break – in which he was supposed to have endured that all-important French test – had been taken up by the fire alarm.

That single powerful punch to break the glass. That's all it had taken. Job done. No French test. No suspension from the school team. *Game on. Genius.*

'Feeling good,' said Kaine. 'Is he here yet? Is he definitely coming?'

'Brian will be here,' said Mr Kerrigan. 'Don't worry about that.'

'Good! I feel strong, man. Got some special skills lined up for him too . . . Oh, sir, if goes well today, can I ask you a favour after the game?'

If the scout did want him to go down to Southampton on Sunday, he was planning to ask whether Mr Kerrigan would be able to give him a lift. He felt sure he would; Mr K always came through for Kaine when he needed him.

'Sure,' said Mr Kerrigan. 'But concentrate on the game and just play your normal style, OK? Terrorize those defenders!'

Kaine nodded. Despite the importance of what was about to happen, he wasn't feeling nervous. Just excited. This was the day he had been waiting for.

When, a few minutes later, the referee put the whistle to his mouth, all Kaine could feel was his heart pumping and his confidence rising.

Taking the kickoff with AJ, he immediately seized possession of the ball and bulldozed past two players in the centre circle. Moving forward, he knocked the ball between the legs of the defensive midfielder and then, just as the two central defenders were surging towards him, he pretended to take on a massive strike before slipping his foot under the ball to conjure a chip instead. He sent his effort spinning towards the top corner. The ball arced high over the goalkeeper . . . only to clip the top of the crossbar and bounce over.

'Ohhh!' Kaine shouted, rubbing his head in frustration but smiling at the same time.

He had come within an inch of opening up the scoring and the opposition had not yet even touched the ball. He just hoped that the scout had arrived on time.

'Hey, Jasmine, hey, Tochi. What time are you guys thinking of getting to the party on the Saturday?' Roxy was so happy that she even felt like being nice to her enemies. She had been walking on air the whole afternoon.

'Oh,' said Tochi. 'We didn't know you were coming.'

'Yeah, I'm coming,' said Roxy breezily. 'AJ'd be really upset if I didn't.'

Roxy jogged away from them over to the tennis court where she was due to meet her dad for training. Finally, AJ had invited her to the party and he'd done it in a great way. Right at the end of lunch, he had come up to her and said: 'Hey, Roxana, maths was a bit boring so I made you this.' Then he'd handed Roxy a piece of paper.

When she had read it, she had done her absolute best not to show any emotion in front of him. *Stay cool, Roxy*, she'd told herself, even though she was desperate to sprint around the playground showing off the note to every single person out there, especially Jasmine and Tochi.

Now she filled her lungs with the fresh air of a warm, sunny day and smiled. Life was good. She'd text AJ later to reply to his invitation. She knew she would still have to find a way of getting to the party without telling her dad, but she'd work that one out. She had to.

While she waited for Daryll, Roxy looked down to the fields below where the football matches were taking place. As soon as she saw Kaine playing and remembered what she had done to his boots, the guilt started rising within her. She also remembered hearing AJ and Kaine discussing the fact that a scout was coming to watch today too. No matter how horrible he had been to her recently, she knew that in cutting his boots, she had crossed the line.

She took out her phone and texted her dad to tell him she would be ten minutes late. Then she ran down to the football fields. She'd cut the boots in such a way that they might not split immediately but, by the end of the game, they would be sure to rip. If she told Kaine now though, he could swap boots with one of the subs before anything happened.

'Kaine!' she shouted as she got to the pitch. 'I need to talk to you.'

She tried to wave him over, but the second he saw her he just turned and looked the other way. She kicked the ground in frustration only to hear her own name being called. She turned round to see her dad marching down towards the pitches.

'Yes, AJ!' Kaine shouted as his best friend received the ball. 'Send me!'

Recognizing the opportunity to release Kaine, AJ clipped a pass into the space behind the defence. Seeing the ball bounce in front of him, everything in Kaine's mind cleared. He scorched across the turf, pulling away from his marker with every rapid stride.

It was a tight angle, but with the goalkeeper rushing out to close him down, Kaine had no hesitation in pulling the ball onto his right foot and unleashing a bullet of a strike. He smashed his foot through the shot, and even though the goalkeeper stretched to his full length to get a firm hand on it, he could not stop the ball from bouncing towards the goal. It was just about to cross the line when, supporting the play from deep, AJ slid in to make sure it got there. He prodded the ball home to open the scoring.

'Yeahhh!' shouted AJ, as he was tumbled to the ground by his celebrating teammates. 'Get in!!'

'Great stuff!' applauded Mr Kerrigan from the sidelines. 'Superb run, Kaine! Great team goal, boys!'

As they jogged back to the halfway line, Kaine ran past his dad, who had now also appeared by the side of the pitch.

'Get off your lazy arse and start moving!' Daryll shouted. 'You should have gone in and finished that off yourself. That should have been your goal!'

Kaine glared at his dad in anger. This big man, with his red face and his pale, white, freckled skin. He wondered how it was even possible that they shared the same blood.

'Lazy!' Daryll shouted again.

Kaine tried not to listen. He was burning with rage, but he did everything he could to hold it in. Not to respond. Today was too important. But then Roxy started shouting and waving at him again too. 'Kaine!' she was yelling. 'Come here! I really need to tell you something right now!'

He snapped. 'Shut up!' he shouted, marching towards them on the touchline. 'Will you both just get lost, you pair of IDIOTS!'

Kaine watched Mr Kerrigan politely suggest to his dad and Roxy that it would be best for everyone if they went and got on with their training up on the tennis court. Seeing his dad and his sister finally disappear, Kaine tried to relax himself and channel his anger back inside his body and turn it into power.

He looked at the man standing next to Mr Kerrigan, making notes in his pad. He was sure that was him. The scout. The one man who could make all his dreams come true in an instant.

Kaine knew he'd played well, but he wanted to show him more. There were only three minutes of the game still to play, and he realized that there was no time left to rely on his teammates to put him centre stage. He was going to have to do it himself.

Dropping into his own half, he nipped in to steal the ball from the opposition attacking midfielder and started dribbling forwards. He hurdled the tackles that flew in on him, he slalomed in between the players who tried to block him, and he outsprinted the defenders who attempted to keep pace with him. He ran with such ferocious speed that he tore a hole right through the centre of the opposing side. He was just drawing his leg back to shoot when he was shoved hard in the back from behind by the last defender.

'Penalty!!' shouted Mr Kerrigan, running up the touchline. 'Got to be!'

The referee nodded and blew his whistle. As soon as he pointed to the spot, AJ – the team's nominated penalty taker – went to collect the ball.

'I'm taking this,' said Kaine, snatching the ball out of AJ's hands.

'I'm on pens, man!' protested AJ, trying to retrieve the ball. 'You know that.'

'You've had your goal,' snapped Kaine, holding onto it. 'This one's mine.' He pushed AJ away with such strength that his best friend almost flew into the air.

'Fine,' shouted AJ. 'If it means that much to you, then take it!'

Kaine shook his head and placed the ball down. He took five paces backwards and drew in a deep breath. He cleared his mind of Roxy and his dad. He blocked out the scout. Right now, it was just him and the ball. That was all.

Hearing the whistle, he pushed himself off the mark and moved confidently towards the ball. One step, two steps, three . . . He planted his left foot firmly into the ground and prepared himself to spring into the strike.

But just as he took his final big stride forward, it happened. He felt his left boot split completely open and his foot slipped out. As he ran, his legs became tangled up. He tried to keep his feet but his desperation to do so only speeded up his fall. He was like a huge building crumbling as he first stumbled, then tumbled towards the ground. He fell, landing stomach first, onto the football.

He could only watch as the ball squirted about an inch to the right before being cleared to safety by the defender. And, with that, the referee blew his full-time whistle. It was over.

'Will you pick me up some honey on your way please, Kaine,' said Mamma. 'My chest is a bit blocked up.'

'Sure,' said Kaine. He was speaking to her on the phone as he walked down to her flat after school. 'But you know I'm going to want some Bajan cooking in return!'

He heard Mamma laughing, which then started her coughing again.

'You know how much I love you, don't you, Kaine,' she said, suddenly sounding completely serious. 'You were sent for me. God was giving me another chance with you. I'll always be here for you, Kaine. Your whole life.'

Kaine looked at his phone quizzically. Mamma was talking strangely, and it was an odd time to have this kind of conversation.

'I know, Mamma,' he said. 'But . . . you won't *always* be here, will you? You can't be.'

'Don't you know that love is the most powerful thing in the world?' she said. 'It never stops. Mine will be here for you for your whole life. No matter what. Always remember that . . .'

'I will,' said Kaine. 'I'm just going into the shop now, Mamma. I'll be at yours in ten minutes.'

Kaine bought the honey and a packet of crisps for himself. Then he strolled on towards his grandmother's flat. When he got there and let himself in, he found her lying on the floor, holding her chest. She was conscious but couldn't speak. She was gasping for air and he could see she was in awful pain.

He dropped everything and rushed to her side.

Mamma grabbed his wrist.

'Help me,' she whispered.

Kaine's mind went blank. He was rooted to the spot as panic seized his body and brain.

'What do I do, Mamma?' he cried. 'Tell me what to do!'

He stood up and spun round in circles. He couldn't think. He knew time was ticking away, but he was paralysed by fear.

He called his mum but she was at work and her phone was off. He called Roxy and his dad, but their phones just kept on ringing and ringing. Neither of them answered. They were playing tennis. He kept on trying, kept on calling them, but they never picked up. He didn't know what else to do. Nothing seemed to be real.

'Wait, Mamma!' he shouted, as he could see her closing her eyes. 'Wait!!'

The more frightened he became, the less his brain worked. He shouted for the neighbours, but no one came. He rang 999.

'It's my grandmother!' he cried down the phone. 'Something's happened. She's not conscious. Flat Two, Normandy House, next to the Compton Estate. Please, come as soon as you can!'

He just kept kissing Mamma, rubbing her forehead, trying to keep her with him . . . but by the time the ambulance got there, he knew it was already too late. They walked in and found Kaine lying on the floor next to his grandmother, holding her limp hand. He just lay there. He refused to move his hand from hers.

The paramedics tried to talk to him and ask him questions, but he couldn't hear anything that they were saying. The only person he wanted to talk to was Mamma. They explained that Mamma had had a heart attack and that she had passed away. They asked him where his parents were. He didn't respond.

As they covered Mamma up and took her away, a numbness descended upon Kaine. All the lights in his world had gone out.

'I'm Kaine Campbell,' said Kaine, reaching out his hand.

As soon as the match had finished, he had taken off his one remaining boot and run over to the scout to introduce himself.

The scout shook his hand and then for a moment he, Kaine and Mr Kerrigan stood in silence. The deadlock was broken when Kaine said: 'Sorry about the penalty, that was a complete muck-up but . . . are you going to sign me?' He just blurted it out. He simply could not wait any longer.

While he waited for the answer, he stood up as tall as he could, hoping to embody the future Premier League star for which the scout was searching.

'Well . . . Kaine,' said the scout, taking out his note-pad. 'I'd like to ask you a couple of questions. Is that OK with you?'

'Sure,' said Kaine. 'You can ask anything you want.'

'The man and the girl you told to . . . go away,' said the scout. 'Who were they?'

'That's my dad and my sister. I don't know what they were doing here.'

'Right . . . and how are you doing at school? Is Mrs Buckland happy with you?'

'I think so . . .' he lied. For a second he was wrong-footed by the scout knowing Mrs Buckland's name.

'Basically I put everything into my football,' he said, changing the subject. 'Every second of every day, that's what I'm thinking about. I've got freestyle skills too, by the way. I can show you some, if you like?'

'No thanks,' said the scout, abruptly putting his notepad away. Then he began walking to his car. He gestured for Kaine to follow him. Kaine gulped as he walked alongside the scout, still holding one boot in his hand.

'At our club,' the scout said, 'we are interested in every aspect of a footballer. Not just their performance on the pitch. Of course, that's a huge part of it, but what we also really need to know is: what are they are like off it? What kind of personality are they? Are they getting good support from home? What are they like at school? What type of people do they hang around with? Can they be relied upon? You see, our view is that we're in the business of producing good people, Kaine. Not just good footballers.'

'Right,' said Kaine, shifting from side to side. It was difficult for him to register all the words. He was still so desperate to know the answer to his original question.

'So, are you going to sign me then?' he said.

'No,' said the scout.

'What?' said Kaine. 'But . . . the penalty was an accident! Apart from that, what else could I have done? I did everything! Tell me how I could I have played better and I'll do it, I promise. Just come and see me play one more ti—'

'I'm sorry to disappoint you but I've made my decision,' said the scout. 'And if you think it was because you missed a penalty then I'm not sure you've understood a single word that I've said.'

The scout opened the door and got into his car. He put his key in the ignition and drove away. Watching the car disappear into the distance, Kaine smacked the ground violently with his boot. Then he threw it as far away as he could manage.

PART 2
KNIFE EDGE

THURSDAY

Mr Kerrigan was sitting at the table in the staffroom during morning break the next day when Mrs Buckland approached him. 'Any idea where your friend Kaine Campbell might have got to?'

'I've not seen him yet this morning, actually,' said Mr Kerrigan, taking a sip from his steaming coffee as he read the latest transfer gossip in the newspaper.

He and Kaine had had the briefest of chats after Brian had left, but it hadn't been an easy conversation. Kaine had been so angry. He simply couldn't understand what he'd done wrong. He had been so furious that he'd said that he never wanted to play football again. Noel Kerrigan shook his head. He wondered whether he had done the right thing calling Brian in the first place.

'He's not turned up for school,' said Mrs Buckland. 'And neither his mum nor his sister know where he is. I'm guessing this might have something to do with the match yesterday?'

'I'm guessing you're right,' said Mr Kerrigan, standing up. 'Leave it with me.'

He grabbed one last gulp of coffee and headed for the staffroom door.

Sheldon Statham had answered Kaine's call on the first ring. It was as though he had been expecting it. It was now 11.15 a.m. and the two of them were sitting opposite one another in Dante's.

'Can I ask you a question?' said Kaine, downing his Coke. 'How come you wear the clothes that you do? You know, the suits and all that?'

'Words are not the only way we have of communicating,' said Sheldon.

Kaine looked at Sheldon's creaseless suit. *Power. Control.*

'Here,' said Sheldon, sliding Kaine an envelope across the table. 'I want you to give this to Ellis Small. Do you know who he is?'

'Yes,' Kaine answered, feeling a shiver of fear run through him.

Ellis Small was the leader of the gang who came from the estate next to Compton. A huge man – about 6 ft 5 inches in height and almost the same in width – Small was a bareknuckle boxer and he wanted his Park Avenue gang to take over the Compton Estate and had made no secret about it.

'Just give him the envelope?' asked Kaine, knowing that if he did this, if he went ahead with it, he would be making a pact with Sheldon Statham that he might never be able to get out of. *The start of always.* He felt sick to the core of his stomach.

Sheldon nodded gravely. 'That's it,' he said. 'Nothing else.'

Kaine thought about how he had felt the day before when the scout had driven off and left him standing there. That scout had killed his football dream.

'I'll do it,' he said.

'Good,' said Sheldon. 'Welcome to the team. Whatever you need or want . . . it shall be done.'

'When do you want me to deliver it?' asked Kaine, picking up the envelope.

'Now,' said Sheldon, revealing a set of perfect, gleaming teeth.

Thursday June 7. Lunch Break.

2 days til the party, 3 days til the County Finals.

AJ texted me last night saying he's really looking forward to seeing me at the party. What does that mean?
Is that how 'friends' text each other? Does he have any
idea what he's doing to me?!!

I told him my secret yesterday. My deep, dark secret
that I'm not sure I even like tennis any more. If I
didn't have the Finals on Sunday, if I didn't have tennis,
there'd be no problem about going to the party. I'd be
free and happy just like everyone else. But Dad would
100% explode if I asked him straight out if I could go to
a party the night before the Finals . . . So I'm going to
have to lie to go.

But why should I have to lie? It's my life! I want my
old life back! I want my friends back! This morning he
weighed me again. I hate it hate it HAAAATTTE
IT! Makes me want to scream. This WAS NOT why I

started playing. I played because I loved hitting the ball. I played because I loved the feeling of ripping a winner. I played because I was in love with the game. But that was when it was mine. Not his.

My head feels like it's spinning and changing all the time. The only thing I know is that all the voices stop when I'm with AJ. He even stood up to Kaine for me and came to see if I was alright after the pig was mean about my body again. I really hope something happens at the party. If it's ever going to happen, it's got to happen then . . .

Kaine was just walking through the estate, thinking about where he could find Ellis Small, when Mr Kerrigan appeared out of nowhere, giving him a fright.

'Funny bumping into you here,' Noel said. 'But last time I looked, this wasn't Compton Academy.'

Kaine stared at the ground. 'Yeah, but I learn more here than I do there.'

'I need you to come back to school with me right now,' said Mr Kerrigan, looking up and down the street.

'Leave it, sir,' Kaine said, feeling in his pocket to check he still had the letter. 'I've got something I need to do now. Just say you couldn't find me, yeah? No one really cares whether I'm there or not.'

'Look,' said Mr Kerrigan. 'I know yesterday was a real kick in the teeth. I get it. And I'm sorry for building up your hopes. Maybe the time wasn't right yet. But the best thing you can do now is use your disappointment as ammunition to work even harder, on and off the pitch, so you're really ready when the next chance comes around.'

Kaine laughed. 'I told you yesterday, sir. I'm done with it. The way that guy treated me, chucking me away like I was a piece of dirt. Nah – I deserve more respect than that. And I know how I'm going to get it.'

'What have you been doing this morning, Kaine? Who have you been speaking to?'

'No one,' said Kaine, looking guiltily at the ground.

'Whatever it is you think you're doing now,' said Mr Kerrigan slowly, 'you need to be extremely careful. There are paths in life, there are choices. And you are at one of those crossroads now . . . Sheldon Statham and people like him, they're not heroes, Kaine. They're the worst thing that could ever happen to you.'

Kaine just shrugged his shoulders. He knew that Sheldon was dangerous, but he liked that. No one disrespected *him*.

'You're not the first person to have ever been rejected, you know,' said Mr Kerrigan. 'Anyone who has ever succeeded in life will tell you they've had to pick themselves up off the floor a thousand times . . . I believe in you, Kaine. But the question is, do *you* believe in you? What kind of life do you think you deserve?'

Kaine just stared at Mr Kerrigan.

'Tell me, Kaine. You don't want to be a footballer any more? Fine. So what do you want to be instead? A gangster? Is that it?'

'I don't know. Leave it, sir. Get out of my face, will you?'

Mr Kerrigan was standing so close Kaine could smell

128

the coffee on his breath. 'No, I won't leave it,' the teacher said, taking another step forward, bringing him even closer to Kaine. He was staring straight into Kaine's eyes. 'What. Do. You. Want?' he asked once more.

'I want to stick it to everyone!' Kaine said. 'All the people that think I'm nothing. I want to shut them down. I want everyone to know who I am . . . no one to take liberties with me . . . I want everyone to show me some respect.'

Kaine just stood there, breathing.

'Good,' said Mr Kerrigan finally. 'Now remember that anger. It's what we feed on when the times get really hard. You *are* going to be someone, Kaine. You are going to be a great footballer . . . *If* you are brave enough to want it.' He looked at his watch. 'Now, I think it's time you and I got back to school, don't you?'

Mr Kerrigan started walking down the street. After a moment's thought, Kaine decided to follow him. He'd let Mr Kerrigan think he'd won this one, but the truth was that nothing had changed in his mind. He would still keep his word to Sheldon and deliver the letter to Ellis Small. He'd do it later and Sheldon would be proud of him.

He would start to get some respect.

As soon as school finished, Kaine went straight to a few of the hangouts he knew and got the information he needed to find Ellis Small. Once he knew where to go, he watched some of the videos that the other boys in the Compton gang had posted online to psych himself up. He was one of them now.

Then he put on his cap and walked through the Park Avenue Estate, keeping his head down so no one would recognize him. Finally, he entered Patten's Boxing Gym with the envelope tucked into his trousers. As he climbed the steps to the weights room, his heart was pounding hard. He was about to come face to face with a very big man. A man who was about to receive a letter containing the words:

> You're not the first person to try to take my manor.
> Do you know what happened to all the others?
> S.S.

Kaine hadn't been able to resist reading the note. He liked the way Sheldon used words, and he tried to remember each new phrase.

Opening the door, he was expecting the weights room to be busy, but it was completely empty apart from Ellis Small, who was at the far end by the mirrors, covered in sweat, bench-pressing the heaviest weights that Kaine had ever seen anyone lift.

For a moment, he stood frozen in awe. He could feel his heart beating in his throat. Was he really going to do this? Was he really going to threaten Ellis Small? He ordered himself to continue and walked across the room. The closer he got, the more sick he felt. What if Ellis Small opened the letter while he was there? What if he grabbed Kaine? Kaine was big for his age, but Ellis Small was a colossus. He would be able to destroy Kaine with one hand.

Finally, Kaine was standing above Ellis Small. Almost unable to breathe, he looked down at the fiercest man he had ever come face to face with. Seeing the onlooker above him, Small set the weights down.

It was now or never. Kaine quickly dropped the envelope onto Ellis Small's chest and said: 'This is from Sheldon. Stay off our turf!'

'What the—' said Ellis Small, but Kaine had already sprinted out of the room, down the stairs and through the front door of the gym before Small had the chance to catch him. As he raced away down the street, Kaine could hear Small shouting at him from the open window on the top floor of the gym: 'I see you, boy! When I catch you, I'm gonna knock your head straight off your shoulders.'

Kaine ran and ran until he was sure he was far enough away not to be caught. He stopped by the side of the road, panting. He bent over and took several huge gulps of air to try to get his breath back. Then he stood up and took off his cap. His head was spinning and his stomach was in knots. For the life of him, he could not remember how or why he'd got himself into this situation. He was sure of one thing though; now Ellis Small knew who he was, he would have to protect himself.

9.30 p.m.

Dad's just given me the big psych-up talk. He says in less than 72 hours we'll be back home holding the County Finals Trophy and that it's just the start. We're going all the way to the top, to Number One in the world.

I nearly did it. I nearly told him that it's not 'we', that it's 'me'. I so nearly told him to back off. I so wanted to. But then I saw that vein in his neck start throbbing and I just couldn't do it. I know he's still so angry and embarrassed ~~not~~ about not having a job, that it'll just take one thing to tip him right over the edge. If he lost it, if he properly lost it, I reckon he could actually tear the whole flat down.

I keep thinking about what he'd do to Kaine if he found out about him setting off the fire alarm. I know it was Kaine. I could tell by one look at his face. He actually doesn't care about anything. He seems to be getting even more cocky by the day. He's started walking around with this sly look on his face like he knows something that we don't.

At least my stupid brother is good for one thing. I know how I'm going to go to the party now. I heard him climbing in through his window on the fire-escape side last night because he didn't want to talk to Mum and Dad when he got home. And it gave me the idea. That's how I'll go to the party – I'll tell Dad I'm having an early night to get proper sleep before the Finals and then I'll climb out my window and get out down the fire escape. Thanks, Kaine!

FRIDAY

'Kaine, I need to talk to you,' said AJ, catching up with him as they walked home after school on Friday. He looked worried.

'What's up?' said Kaine.

'It's Rufus Blackstock,' said AJ. 'He's still got it in for you, you know? He was going all around the estate looking for you last night, saying that he hadn't forgotten what you said about his mum and that he's going to do you.'

'So?' said Kaine.

'Aren't you scared? I heard he's got in with Ellis Small. Don't you just want to make things OK before it gets out of hand?'

Part of Kaine wanted to tell AJ everything. There was so much he didn't know. After doing his job with Ellis Small the previous night, Kaine had called Sheldon and told him that he'd changed his mind about the knife. That he understood he needed to protect himself now. He'd met Sheldon and picked it up before he'd gone home. Then he'd crawled through the window by the fire escape so that no one would ask him any questions when he got in . . . He wished he could tell AJ the truth . . . but there were some things he just wouldn't understand.

'Rufus needs to watch himself,' said Kaine, trying to laugh it off. 'Everyone knows the Compton gang are in charge around here. Sheldon Statham's clever, man. I heard he's gonna destroy Ellis Small and anyone's that's with him.' He felt the outline of the folded weapon in his trouser pocket as they strode forward. 'And if Rufus tries to come for me, I'll make him sorry he was born.'

They were just walking into the chicken shop when Queenie galloped up alongside them.

'Word up, guys,' he said, his face bright red from running. 'Listen, I've been thinking . . . At the party, will you both try really hard to set me up with a girl, please?'

'You don't need our help with girls, Queenie,' said Kaine. 'They love boys like you. All your sensitivity and stuff. That's what they go for.'

'Guaranteed,' AJ chipped in.

'Thanks, guys,' said Queenie, who was noticeably watching Kaine walk and trying to copy the way he moved as they made their way down the street. 'I mean, you know I play the big man an' all with my bredren in my hood. But, to tell you the absolute truth, I've never actually kissed a girl. I haven't even had one over to my crib yet. Give me some advice, fam. Please. I'm desperate here. Do I have a sign on my head that says *Friend-Zone me*?!'

'Just be yourself, Queenie,' said AJ, laughing. 'It'll happen, man. My mum says there's a lid for every pot.'

'I'll try my best,' said Queenie, sloping off home. 'But please, guys, remember me at the party. I just . . . really want a shawty.'

After he'd gone, Kaine and AJ looked at each other and cracked up.

'Classic Queenie!' said AJ. 'We definitely have to get our boy a kiss at the party!'

Kaine gave AJ a fistbump to show that he agreed. 'You got everything you need?' he asked.

'Killed it,' said AJ. 'Just need some more speakers. Want both rooms bouncing.'

'Speakers? Don't worry,' said Kaine, trying to remember the exact words that Sheldon had used when he'd started working for him. 'It shall be done,' he said finally, smiling at how much he liked the sound of the words as they came out of his mouth.

It was 7.15 p.m. and Samantha Campbell had just finished laying the table for dinner.

She went back to the cooker and smelled the food. As she did so, she saw the picture frame on the windowsill. She'd taken the family photo out of it and asked Roxy to show it to Kaine the other night when they'd had an argument. She'd hoped that looking at the photo of themselves might have triggered a reaction in the kids. The frame was still empty.

She found herself wondering at what point it had all changed. She remembered the twins doing everything together as toddlers, how they used to search and long for one another when they were separated. They even had that special twin-ability connection, knowing what the other was thinking. It was real. They truly loved each other and if either of them was in any kind of pain, the other had been able to feel it too. That was how close they had been. She was sure that it was still there. That underneath everything they still had that special bond, but somewhere along the way things had gone wrong.

How? Why? They were the questions that tormented her.

She dipped the wooden spoon into the sauce and

tasted it. Not quite as good as her mother's but not bad at all. The flavours brought back memories of her own childhood and the relationship she'd had with her brother. She couldn't remember any rivalry. She had worshipped the ground Anthony had walked on, and he had been her protector, always making sure that she was safe and happy.

'It's ready,' she called, filling each of the bowls with rice and putting the huge saucepan of fish on the table for people to dig in and help themselves. Salt fish and cou-cou was something that they all enjoyed, and this Friday evening she hoped it would please one of the clan in particular. She had still not been able to save up the money for Kaine's birthday present, and for that, each day she felt a stinging guilt deep inside.

At least he'd stopped talking about needing to be in Southampton at the weekend. Making choices like who the car should be used for carved her heart in two.

Soon the table was full of all four Campbells busily munching their way through the dish, which, she knew, was as close as she was going to get to them saying: *Thanks, Mum, for spending all that time preparing this lovely meal. We really appreciate it.*

She allowed herself a moment of pride. Yes, they had their problems, but so did everyone. They were a unit, she told herself. They stuck together and, underneath the difficulties, they all loved each other. She had a loyal husband doing his best at a really difficult time. She knew he didn't always know how to show it in the right way, but he cared about his family more than anything. He was a good man, and together, they had the two most beautiful children in the world. She was a lucky woman.

'Can I propose a little toast,' she said, raising her glass into the air. 'To us. To the Campbells.'

Roxy lifted her glass and Samantha noticed, to her surprise, that Kaine did too. He had a strange smile on his face. One that she had not seen before.

'And, good luck to Roxy for Sunday,' added Daryll. 'The journey is about to begin!'

Samantha once again looked at Kaine. Even though they were toasting Roxy, he was still smiling, as though he knew something they didn't.

'Can you take that stupid cap off while we're having dinner,' Daryll suddenly said to Kaine.

'Get a job, mate,' said Kaine. 'Then I'll start taking orders from you!'

'Stop it, both of you. Just be quiet,' said Samantha in a loud, clear voice. 'We are not arguing tonight. I've had enough. That's it.'

For a second, the table went silent. Both Kaine and Daryll lowered their heads.

'Now,' she continued. 'Tonight we are going to have a calm and happy dinner like a normal family. OK?'

No one answered back. She was just about to return to her meal when her phone rang. 'You lot carry on, before it gets cold,' she said, moving towards the sofa to take the call.

'Hello?' she said. 'Hello . . . Yes, yes . . . I see . . .' Samantha was listening intently, staring at Kaine. She held onto the phone tightly to stop herself from dropping it. 'Yes, of course,' she said, trying to keep her voice as even as possible. 'We'll see you then.'

She put the phone back down and retook her seat at the table. For a few seconds she didn't say anything. She just listened to the sound of clinking cutlery.

'Who was it?' asked Daryll finally.

'It was Mrs Buckland,' said Samantha, looking up at her son. 'Kaine set off the fire alarm at school on Wednesday. She wants to see us first thing on Monday morning. I think they're going to exclude him.'

Friday June 8. 9 p.m.
1 day until the party
2 days until County Finals . . .

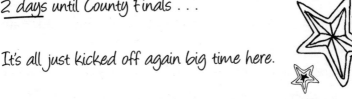

It's all just kicked off again big time here.

School found out about Kaine and the fire alarm and now they might expel him. Mrs Buckland called and it went nuclear. Kaine thought that I had ratted him out (which I hadn't). He called me a snitch and went for me. Then Dad got involved and told Kaine not to dare lay a finger on me and then those two squared up and I actually thought they were going to have a proper fight until Mum broke them up . . . In the end Kaine stormed out and said he hated us all and that he was never coming back.

Mum took it all really seriously and kept asking how he could use the word 'hate' about us. She never seems to get it. Kaine just uses the words that he thinks will hurt the most. Let's see how long he stays away for. I give it 24 hours at the most.

Kaine texted Sheldon as soon as he got down to the estate car park, and within what seemed like seconds, the BMW pulled up. The soothing breeze of the air conditioning in the car immediately made him feel calmer and more secure.

'I need a favour,' Kaine said. 'I'm not going back home. Ever. I need somewhere to stay.'

Sheldon smoked his cigar and looked at Kaine for a long time without saying anything. Then he reached out and lightly touched Kaine's cheek with his hand. 'You're just like me,' he whispered.

'So . . .' said Kaine. 'You haven't answered me. Can you help me?'

'The answer that I give to you is doing it,' said Sheldon. He put out his cigar and reached into his jacket pocket, producing a set of keys which he placed in Kaine's hand.

'Thank you, Sheldon,' Kaine said. 'Thank you so much.'

'Not everything in life is quite as it seems,' said Sheldon. 'You asked for the blade, not to hurt but to protect yourself. Likewise, those that like to paint me as the devil are wrong. People come to me with their problems, and I solve them. Does that sound like the devil to you?'

Kaine shook his head.

'I started with nothing and no one, just like you,' said Sheldon, 'and now the whole of Compton is my family . . . I protect everyone. Including you.'

'I want to be a boss like you,' Kaine said.

Sheldon smiled. 'The pupil always wants to imitate the master. Are you telling me you want to join us for good, Kaine?'

'Yeah,' said Kaine, nodding. 'Yeah, I do.'

SATURDAY

'Hey,' said AJ, opening the door to Kaine. 'It's only five o'clock. I wasn't expecting you this early!'

Kaine was extra happy to see his friend. It had been a rough night. Everything had been OK when he was in the car. He had felt sure about what he was doing. Clear that leaving home was his only option. But when Sheldon had given him some cash and left him at an empty flat on the edge of the estate, he had felt weird straightaway. Hearing people shouting and screaming in the flat next door and realizing that he was completely alone and that Rufus or Ellis – or, worse still, both – could come and get him at any time, he'd spent the whole night wide awake, with his hand gripped tightly around the knife.

In the morning, ignoring the stream of texts and voicemail messages from his mum asking where he was, he'd gone straight to the shopping centre until the time was right to head to AJ's to get set up for the party. Just being with AJ immediately made things feel normal again, and he had bought something at the shopping centre that he knew would put a smile on his friend's face.

'This is for tonight,' said Kaine, reaching into his pocket and pulling out a wireless speaker.

'Nice one!' said AJ. 'Where did you get that?'

'Finally got my birthday present,' said Kaine. *Just a shame I had to buy it for myself*, he thought.

AJ connected his phone to the speaker and put on a track.

'Turn it up full!' said Kaine.

AJ put the speaker on maximum volume and the whole flat began to reverberate with the sound. One of the cups even fell off the table and smashed on the floor. The boys looked at each other and started laughing. Kaine posted a photo of them together online with the tag: *Epic party – About to begin!*

It was 8.45 p.m. and Roxy was nearly ready. Half an hour before, she'd gone into the lounge where her dad was watching TV, put on a fake yawn and said that she was going to get a good early night so that she would be full of energy for the Finals in the morning.

'Good girl,' he'd said. 'Wise decision.'

Then she'd gone into her room and got changed. She'd tried on several outfits, eventually settling for one that she thought showed off the best part of her body, her flat stomach. She looked at herself in the mirror and took in a gulp of air. On the court, sometimes, when she was on top form, she knew she could control everything, especially her opponent. But real life wasn't so simple. She knew there was nothing that she could do to control the way she looked, and she knew she would never be as beautiful as Jasmine or as confident as Tochi.

She opened her window and looked across the estate. She'd been able to hear the music coming from AJ's flat since around 5 p.m. that afternoon. Before crawling out of the window and onto the fire escape, she decided to have a quick look at people's photos online to see what everyone else was wearing. She felt nervous and wanted to make sure her outfit wouldn't make her stand out in a bad way.

She opened her account and clicked straight onto Kaine's profile, @KingKaineCampbell. Although her mum had been going mad all day because Kaine hadn't come home the night before, Roxy knew he was fine and was definitely at the party. Sure enough, a collection of photos from Kaine at the party filled her screen. She scrolled down them until one caught her eye. She opened it and then spread her fingers to enlarge it. It was a selfie Kaine had taken, but in the background, Roxy could clearly make out the image of Tochi, who had draped herself over AJ and was kissing him on the cheek.

Roxy felt as though she had been stabbed in the heart. She thought she was going to vomit. She collapsed onto her bed and started punching her pillow. Of course – it made sense now. This had been Tochi's plan all week. She was going to wait until Roxy arrived and then she was going to kiss AJ right in front her. Roxy just knew it. She could imagine AJ giving her that same regretful smile he'd given her the other day when he'd left her in the playground to go and look at Jasmine and Tochi's temporary tattoos. Just thinking about it made her feel sick to the core. Well, there was no way she was going to give Tochi the satisfaction of doing that to her in front of everyone at the party.

From her bedside table, she took out the note that AJ had given her at school – the one that she had treasured so much. She drew a circle in a specific place and then took a photo of what she had done. She felt so sad and angry as she texted it to him. Feeling the rage at both Tochi and AJ beginning to rise up even further inside her, she dropped to the floor and did the only thing she felt her muscly body was good for: fifty press-ups.

The party was in full swing and the bass was banging so hard that conversation was close to impossible. Not that it mattered. Kaine had already decided that this was going to be a very good night. Jasmine was looking hot, and they had exchanged a couple of glances across the room. He hadn't talked to her yet, but he would do it later. He was happy with the way his hair was shaping and his body felt good. Sometimes his bones just felt right, and tonight was one of those nights.

'Your sis looks like she's a no-show then?' said AJ.

'What?' said Kaine.

'I said, do you know where Roxy is?' AJ was now shouting in order to be heard above the pulsating beat. 'She said she was coming!'

But just before Kaine could lay into his friend again about staying away from his sister, there was a commotion at the door. Kaine looked across and saw that Rufus was there with three other big lads, and they were trying to force their way in.

Rufus was pointing angrily at Kaine. 'I told you you was dead!' he was yelling. 'And now you definitely are. Ellis is after you too now. I showed him a picture of you on my phone and he recognized you! You're done, mate! Done!'

Kaine felt his hand twitch and reach towards his knife, which was in his trouser pocket.

'We don't want any trouble,' AJ shouted. He and a few of the other boys were trying to close the door and he was gesturing for his older brother to come over and help. 'And we're only letting in people who were invited.'

Kaine could feel his whole body shaking, and he kept his hand right by his knife in case Rufus and his crew managed to burst through. Rufus was still shouting and swearing at Kaine. He had a crazed look in his eye.

It took AJ, his brother and five of the other boys all pushing together to shut the door on them. Finally they managed to close it, only for Rufus to start kicking the door down from the outside.

'I'm calling the police right now!' AJ's brother shouted from behind the door.

Rufus gave the door one last big kick. Then, as he went, he banged on the window and pointed at Kaine, making a throat-slitting gesture. It was the same gesture he'd made when Kaine had first started winding him up about his mum on the football court the previous weekend.

With everyone now looking at him, Kaine tried to smile and pretend that he wasn't bothered, but his entire body had gone into a state of shock. He could feel himself being dragged deeper and deeper . . . closer to danger by the day. Now he was almost drowning in it.

9.15 p.m.

I didn't go to the party. I know that AJ's going to kiss Tochi. I just know it and I couldn't watch it. It makes me feel sick just thinking about it. I know I won't sleep tonight. Thinking about them — and the Finals tomorrow. Biggest tournament of my life. So why do I feel like I don't <u>even</u> want to play? I just wish I could disappear and no one could ever find me again. And, you know what? If I did, no one would even miss me.

Once he was sure Rufus had gone, Kaine had gone into the bathroom to get his head straight. To think. If it was true that Rufus was now working with Ellis Small, and they were both after him, he was in very big trouble. He clenched his teeth and tried to stay calm. He'd call Sheldon first thing in the morning to tell him what had happened. Sheldon would protect him. He would know what to do . . .

He splashed water on his face and looked at himself in the mirror. Then he went back out into the heaving throng of bodies in the main room. Tonight was about the party, and he needed to start enjoying himself. He connected his phone to the speaker. Hearing the music stop, everyone looked around and started booing. But then Kaine's tunes properly kicked in. He watched proudly as the party started jumping. AJ had hired party lights too, which were throwing all shades of colours onto the makeshift dancefloor, making everyone want to get up and move even more.

A whole group of people were now in a circle clapping Queenie, who was in the centre doing the strangest dance Kaine had ever seen. Wearing a fluorescent yellow headband, his face was beetroot red and sweat was pouring down his face. He was pumping out his arms from side to side and stamping down his feet as though he was putting out an imaginary fire. Kaine pushed his way through the crowd until he got to AJ, and as soon as they saw each other, they fell down laughing.

Kaine had so much adrenaline and nervous energy flowing through him, he felt light-headed and dizzy. He was laughing so much he was almost in a daze. He hoisted AJ to his feet and they moved to join in with the clapping crowd. Then Kaine gave AJ the nod. Entering the circle together, they both gave Queenie a high-five to relieve him of his duties, then fistbumped each other. Now it was time for the boys to go to work.

To the sound of all their favourite songs, they broke out every one of their best moves, and as the circle around the boys got bigger, the applause got louder too. Kaine nodded confidently in time to the beat. Just like the football field, this was his domain. He knew his steps inside out, and he knew there was no one that could move like him.

With one final backflip, he and AJ did a synchronized mime of a mic drop, before leaving the circle to a major ovation from their crowd. The applause continued for some time before Queenie made his way back into the centre and attempted a caterpillar that never quite got off the ground.

'Not bad,' said Jasmine as Kaine walked over to get a drink. 'Almost as good as my brother.'

Kaine smiled. 'Yeah? Your brother got moves, has he?' he asked, helping himself to some ice. He was so happy to be talking to her but still hadn't looked her in the eye.

'Yeah,' said Jasmine. 'He's a great dancer. For a five-year-old.'

They both laughed.

'Oh no,' said Jasmine, pointing at Kaine's shirt. 'You've got something on your—'

As he went to look down, she flicked him on the chin, saying: 'Sucker!!!'

They laughed again but she still wasn't finished.

'I don't know what you're looking so happy with yourself for,' she said. 'My abs are way harder than yours. Look, feel.' She took Kaine's hand and made his fingers prod her stomach through her T-shirt. 'You wish you had abs like that!'

Kaine smiled and took a step back to look at Jasmine. When she had grabbed his hand he had felt an electricity charge through his body. 'I like your chat.' He smiled. It was the smile he practised in the mirror. His killer smile. Now he looked at her.

'I like *you*,' said Jasmine.

They stared at each other and, almost in slow motion, took a step towards one another. Kaine placed his hand on Jasmine's waist. It felt the most natural thing in the world. He leaned in to her.

At that moment, a song finished and another track on his playlist started up. It took Kaine a couple of seconds to recognize it, but as soon as heard the words his whole body froze.

'Don't look at me now; don't tell me those sacred lies . . .'

As he listened to Mamma's favourite song, every bit of strength drained from him. All of a sudden he could barely stand up straight. He pulled his lips away just as they were about to meet Jasmine's. 'I've . . . got to go,' was all he could manage. He pushed his way through the crowd and left the party.

As he sprinted down the steps of the estate and ran towards Sheldon's empty flat, he needed Mamma's advice more than he had ever done. He knew that she would be so angry at him for having the knife and for being involved with Sheldon – but what choice did he have? People were after him. They wanted to do him serious harm. How else was he supposed to protect himself?

He looked up at the sky and tried to search for the stars, but he couldn't find any. All he could see was darkness and danger. He sensed Ellis or Rufus waiting for him around every corner. He grabbed his knife, stabbing the invisible shadows as he ran.

SUNDAY

Roxy woke up and, with her hands tingling with nerves, put on her tennis kit. Then she went into the kitchen to get breakfast. Her mum was already there, sitting at the table. She looked awful, and Roxy could immediately tell that she hadn't slept all night.

'No sign of him?' asked Roxy.

Her mum shook her head. 'It's been two nights now. I don't know what to think. I've just called work and told them that I can't leave the flat until I know he's safe.'

'He'll be back later today. I know he will,' said Roxy, giving her a hug. 'He just wants to give you both a fright. You know what he's like.'

Then her dad appeared, fully kitted out in his own

coaching gear. 'Let's go, Roxy,' he said. 'Time to put the plan into action.'

They were just getting into the car when Roxy's phone buzzed. She had a new message:

> Really sorry you couldn't come last night. You were the whole reason I had the party in the first place!
> I have a question I want to ask you...
> It's been on my mind for ages...
> Can we talk some time?
> Wishing you good luck for today.
> You know I believe in you.
> AJ x

Roxy felt so light it was almost as though her body was being lifted into the air. She had to read the message five or six times to make sure it was real. This was what she had been waiting for. She knew what AJ wanted to ask her and she knew her answer would be *yes . . . a million—*

'What are you smiling about, Roxy?' said Daryll. 'Today you need to be one hundred per cent focused. Winning should be the only thing in your head.'

Roxy didn't respond. Not even her dad could ruin how she felt right now.

Kaine woke up on a sofa and looked up at the ceiling. The light was streaming in through the window, which had no curtains. For a moment, he had no idea where he was. He got up and felt his neck, which ached from the position he'd been lying in. His phone was dead. He picked up the landline phone that was on the table, but that was dead too.

He felt the panic rise within him again. It had been there since he had left the party the night before and it had continued into his dreams too. He had had the same nightmare repeatedly during the night. He was a fly caught in a web. He struggled to free himself, but the more he tried to escape the more entangled he became. Then three spiders started to converge on him. The spiders had the faces of Rufus, Ellis and Sheldon. They crawled towards him from all directions with their fangs out. He couldn't move. He could only watch as they got closer and closer. They were about to start eating him . . . and that would be the moment that Kaine would wake up, drenched in a cold sweat. It would take him ages to calm down and fall asleep again, only for the same nightmare to restart from the beginning.

He rubbed his cheeks vigorously and shook his head.

He needed to get out of this world, out of this web, before it was too late. He took the knife out of his trousers and looked at it. He pressed its point with his thumb to check its sharpness. It cut straight through his skin, surprising him. Now blood was starting to snake down his arm. Seeing his own blood, he could hear Mamma's voice . . . *Once the first drop is shed* . . .

He stared at the knife again and shook his head. He picked up an old newspaper from the table and carefully wrapped up the blade within it. Then he shoved it in the very bottom of the rubbish bin under the sink, where he hoped it wouldn't be found. He never wanted to see it ever again. Then he walked out of the door and headed for home.

Roxy made her way into the changing rooms, found a locker and put her stuff away.

It was the first moment she'd had by herself to respond to AJ, but as she was about to message him, an uneasy feeling come over her. She wasn't sure why or what it was about, but suddenly Kaine's face came into her mind. He looked in pain. He looked in danger. Unnerved, Roxy took out her phone and quickly typed a text to AJ.

> Yes, we can talk.
> I have some things I need to say
> to u too.

Then she sent him another text straight after.

> Also, this may sound weird, but
> can u make sure K's ok today?
> I have this strange feeling...and
> just need to know he's ok.
> Will call u when I get home
> (with the trophy)
> Rx

Although it was hard, Roxy knew she had to try and put her thoughts of both AJ and Kaine out of her mind. There was nothing more she could do about either of

them right now. The matches were just about to begin.
It was time to start concentrating on her tennis.

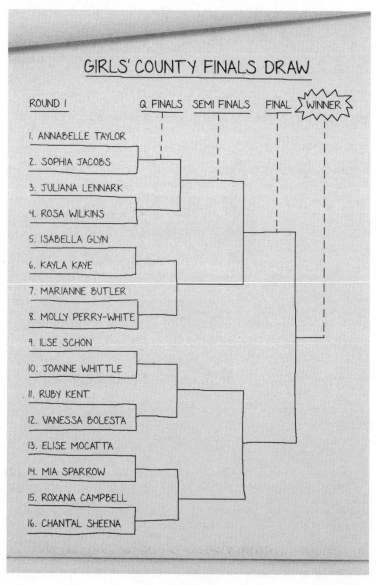

GIRLS' COUNTY FINALS DRAW

ROUND 1   Q FINALS   SEMI FINALS   FINAL   WINNER

1. ANNABELLE TAYLOR

2. SOPHIA JACOBS

3. JULIANA LENNARK

4. ROSA WILKINS

5. ISABELLA GLYN

6. KAYLA KAYE

7. MARIANNE BUTLER

8. MOLLY PERRY-WHITE

9. ILSE SCHON

10. JOANNE WHITTLE

11. RUBY KENT

12. VANESSA BOLESTA

13. ELISE MOCATTA

14. MIA SPARROW

15. ROXANA CAMPBELL

16. CHANTAL SHEENA

While Roxy considered her route to the final, she went to the mirror to make sure her hair was right and to put on some sun lotion. Behind her, she heard a familiar laugh.

'Don't tell me you're actually still wearing those things!' said Annabelle Taylor, standing next to Roxy and pointing at her trainers. 'If you want to be a serious player, you should at least try and look the part.'

'Is that the best you've got?' said Roxy. 'Is that supposed to put me off?'

'I'm not trying to put you off,' said Annabelle. 'I just feel sorry for you.' She was tying her long blonde hair into a ponytail.

'Well, I feel sorry for *you*,' said Roxy. 'Because no matter how much money you spend on clothes and flying out to train in America you'll never be able to buy style . . . or talent.'

'It's just a shame,' said Annabelle, shaking her head. 'I took a whole load of my old trainers to the charity shop last week. If I'd have known, you could have had a pair of those.'

Roxy watched Annabelle stride out onto the courts like she was a member of the Royal Family. *You just made one very big mistake, Annabelle Taylor*, she said to herself. *This tournament is now on. It is so ON.*

Kaine walked into the chicken shop and put the exact money down for a king chicken fillet and chips.

'Kaine!' said Sami, coming out from the back with a bucketful of drumsticks. He looked worried. 'There was a boy in here before. He was asking questions about you, asking where were you. I didn't tell him nothing. You are my friend. But he looked angry. Be careful, OK?'

Kaine nodded and ate his food in record time. He could feel the web closing in on him with every passing second. He had to get home quickly. But there was one thing he needed to do first. He went into the convenience shop and picked up a bunch of flowers for his mum. They were exactly the kind she liked. He smelled them as he walked towards the door. They smelled like a new start.

'There!!' someone shouted as he left the shop. 'There he is!'

Kaine turned around to see Rufus's face right behind him, three bigger boys were with him. He instantly dropped the flowers and started running down the street. If he could get back to the estate he'd be able to find somewhere to hide. He weaved in and out of passersby, sprinting as fast as he could. He looked around to see how far in front of them he was, and in that momentary second, as he took his eye off where he was running, he thudded straight into a brick wall of a man.

Stunned, Kaine looked up and saw Ellis Small in front of him. He froze.

'You better watch where you're going, boy,' said Small, revealing two gold teeth as he spoke. 'You could get your head knocked off your shoulders running around like that.'

Kaine turned to run the other way, but Rufus and his gang had now caught up with him. He was trapped.

'Go on, Ellis!' shouted Rufus. 'Do him!'

Then, right there, in the middle of the street, Ellis Small grabbed Kaine by the neck and lifted him completely off the ground. He held him in the air as though he were the weight of a little puppy. People on the street could see what was happening. With his eyes, Kaine pleaded with them to do something, to call for help. But they just looked the other way. Small, still holding Kaine in the air, dragged him down a little side alley.

'You think you can threaten me?' said Ellis Small, tightening his grip around Kaine's windpipe. 'You think you can come to *my gym* and tell me to stay off *your* turf? This is *my* turf! When I'm finished with you, Sheldon and everyone else is gonna know it.'

Kaine's pushes and punches bounced off Ellis Small. He kicked out, but Rufus grabbed his legs and restrained them.

'Park Avenue runs this area now,' shouted Rufus, punching Kaine in the stomach. 'And this is what you get for talking about my mum!'

Kaine wanted to scream for help, but no sound was coming out of his mouth. As each moment passed, Ellis squeezed his throat even harder, and the oxygen could no longer get to Kaine's lungs.

His struggles went from desperate to slow and then, finally, to limp.

Roxy was powered by pure anger. The tournament was about one thing only now: reaching the final and putting Annabelle Taylor firmly in her place. She was smashing aside anyone that was in her way.

'Any word from Mum or Kaine yet?' she asked her dad as they walked off court following a 6–2, 6–1 demolition of her semi-final opponent. Although she was playing near faultless tennis, the uneasy feeling about Kaine had remained with her and, if anything, started to intensify.

'No,' said Daryll. 'Mum's called the police to let them know that he's missing, but I think she's overreacting. Try to forget that. We need you to stay focused on this final.' He stopped walking and brought his head down so that it was level with Roxy's. 'You do not let that girl Annabelle beat you,' he said. 'Whatever you have to do to beat her, you do it. Winning is all that matters. Do you hear me?'

Roxy nodded, but inside she wanted to scream. He was suffocating her again. She almost couldn't breathe.

Kaine held out for as long as he could. Gasping in little bits of air, he had been able to stay conscious for several minutes while Ellis Small squeezed and shook his neck. But now he could feel his body begin to give up. His brain started to separate itself from his physical pain. His bloodshot eyes became fixed on a flower petal on the pavement. He could see his mum in the kitchen, waiting for him. He didn't want her to feel more pain. He just wanted to her to be happy. He had just wanted to give her the flowe—

'Put the boy down.'

Kaine was barely alive. He could only just hear the words. They sounded muffled, like they were coming from far away.

'Jog on, mate, otherwise you'll be next,' responded Ellis. He squeezed Kaine's throat even harder.

'I said: "Put the boy down",' repeated the voice, which from the depths of his lingering consciousness, Kaine recognized.

There was more shouting and then Kaine heard the voice say: 'Yes, I know exactly who you are. And so do the police, who are on the other end of this line.'

Kaine could feel the blood vessels in his eyes were about to pop, but he tried hard to focus them. He saw

Mr Kerrigan standing in front of Ellis Small, with his arm outstretched, showing him his phone.

'The police are on their way right now,' Mr Kerrigan was saying.

'Who the hell are you?' demanded Small.

'I'm the boy's teacher,' responded Mr Kerrigan. 'And I reckon you've got about two minutes before they get here.'

Kaine felt himself being dropped to the ground and being caught by Mr Kerrigan. He vaguely saw the others scattering in different directions. They were shouting things at him, but he couldn't hear properly. He now saw that AJ was there too.

'You OK?' Mr Kerrigan asked Kaine, holding him in his arms.

'I . . . think so,' said Kaine weakly.

'Good,' said Mr Kerrigan. 'The police will be here in a minute.'

'Sir,' said Kaine. 'I don't want the police involved . . . I just want to go home.'

Roxy watched as another of Annabelle's atomic first serves whizzed past her. She didn't even move. There was no point. Roxy had come out and started the match in top form, seizing the first set, but since then, since Annabelle had got her serve going, it had become an annihilation.

The score was now one set all and 5–2, *15–love* to Annabelle. Roxy was on the verge of defeat. There was nothing she could do to stem the string of aces that were raining down on her. Under the gathering dark, heavy clouds, Annabelle's shots resembled a stream of fluorescent missiles. And when Roxy wasn't being destroyed on the court, her dad was peppering her with orders from the sideline.

'Take it earlier! . . . How can you miss that? . . . Never hit the net. NEVER!!' It was endless – and in front of everyone who was watching too. She wrestled with her thoughts and tried to regain her concentration. She even thought about walking off the court. But she couldn't let Annabelle win that way, or her dad for that matter.

Roxy waited for Annabelle's next service. The delay while Annabelle kept bouncing the ball, was interminable. It was as though she was waiting to serve as long as possible to prolong Roxy's agony. Roxy looked down at the ground and reached within herself for something, anything, to hang onto. She was stranded in the middle of an ocean, and there was a storm blowing at her from all sides. She needed a lifeboat to keep her alive.

Annabelle bounced the ball for the sixth time and then sent one of her straight-down-the-middle aces flying past Roxy. Thirty–love. Roxy steadied herself once more. She was not dead yet. She was still searching. Looking for one crack of light to allow her a way back.

She swayed from side to side. Her reflexes were ready, just waiting for the starter gun. She watched Annabelle bounce the ball once, twice . . . three, four . . . five times before sending down one of her topspinning, high-kicking, angled serves. It drove Roxy so far out wide that, although she managed to just about return the ball, Annabelle was already there, waiting at the net, to clip the volley away for another winner.

Match point to Annabelle.

With the atmosphere darkening further, Roxy trudged back to her position and took up her returning stance. She watched as Annabelle once again bounced the ball five times and threw it into the air. This time Roxy gambled. Without waiting for the serve to be struck, she took three steps to her right, anticipating another topspin serve to her forehand. Sure enough, down it came. Roxy watched it arc towards exactly where she was already standing. She had all the time in the world to ready herself to return it. She adjusted her feet, drew back her racket and ripped a seismic return straight down the line past Annabelle before she had even arrived at the net. Annabelle watched in shock as the winner whizzed past her.

'About time!' Daryll shouted, leaping up from his seat.

Roxy clenched her fist and went back to the baseline, ready to receive once more. Had she been right or was it just a fluke? She watched carefully as Annabelle now bounced the ball four times and tossed it skywards. This time, Roxy moved even earlier. She took a step to her left and waited for the straight-down-the-middle serve. When it came, Roxy was there, ready for it, crashing back a perfectly timed, doubled-handed top-spin, cross-court return. It had power, it had angle and it had pace. It was a killer. Annabelle looked completely confused as it roared past her.

And she continued to carry that expression as Roxy went on to win four out of the next five games. She had detected the most simple but crucial 'tell'. If Annabelle bounced the ball an even number of times, she was going down the middle to Roxy's backhand. If she bounced it an odd number of times, she was going out wide to the forehand. It had taken the whole match to unlock it, and no one else had noticed it, but Roxy knew she had done it. She had cracked the code of Annabelle's serve. And now she had that foreknowledge of what was about to come, she could gain that vital extra second and make sure she was always there waiting, taking the return earlier and earlier and striking her shots harder and harder.

Living in a zone of excellence, Roxy stormed back to 6–6, forcing the deciding set into a tie-break.

'Any news from Kaine?' Roxy asked her dad at the second change of ends. The breaker itself was now locked at six–all.

'He's OK. Mum just texted.'

'Good,' said Roxy, taking a moment to sit in her chair and wipe her face with her towel. She knew that AJ would've made sure that Kaine was all right. She couldn't wait to call him after the match. Just thinking about the text he'd sent gave her such a warm feeling inside. They had so much to talk about. And so much to look forward to.

'What are you doing?' growled Daryll. 'Don't you dare show her you're tired. Get up now and win this match!'

Hearing his words, feeling his pressure, Roxy felt something inside her snap. She had been pushed too far. She stood up and walked over to her dad and, in front of all the people who were watching, she said: 'Will you just BACK OFF!'

There was silence. Even Roxy was shocked to hear the words come out of her mouth.

'Be quiet and listen to me,' said Daryll. 'I know how t—'

'No!' said Roxy. 'You listen to me! You are driving me mad! . . . Now, I *am* going to win this match . . . and I *am* going to beat her, but I'm not doing it for you. I'm doing it *for me*!'

Everyone turned to look at Daryll. Roxy could see his eyes widen and the vein in his neck start to throb. She didn't know how he was going to react. Then, finally, he said: 'OK . . . go do what you need to do.'

After they had given Kaine a few minutes to get himself together, Mr Kerrigan and AJ slowly lifted Kaine to his feet.

'I've just spoken to your mum,' said Mr Kerrigan. 'She's waiting for you at home.'

Kaine smiled. He knew in that moment that he never wanted to make his mum worried again. It had been so close. If it hadn't been for Mr K and AJ . . . It didn't bear thinking about.

'How . . . come . . . you were here, sir?' asked Kaine as they slowly started to walk. Mr Kerrigan and AJ were supporting him on either side.

'You can thank AJ for that,' said Mr K.

'And you can thank your sister for *that*,' said AJ. 'She texted me asking me to make sure you were all right. She was worried about you.'

Kaine felt like crying. After everything that had happened, after all the arguments they'd had, it was Roxy who had saved him. She must have known. She must have sensed that he was in trouble. That connection between them, still there, after all this time.

They carried on walking in silence, but they had only got ten metres down the street when Kaine suddenly stopped and held his head in his hands. He felt the most terrible pain in his brain.

'What's happened, Kaine?' asked Mr Kerrigan. 'What's wrong?'

'Sir!' said Kaine, clutching his teacher's wrist. 'Roxy!'

Roxy looked up to the sky and saw that the black, ominous clouds were about to break. As they parted to allow the sun to shine through, Roxy realized that her pounding head had stopped hurting. Now she had told her dad to give her some space, it was as though all the pressure that she'd been feeling had been released. She was able to think clearly. More clearly than she had been able to for a long time. Perhaps ever.

'Let's do this,' Roxy said to herself. She walked back out to the centre of the court.

'I want this,' she said out loud so everyone could hear. 'I *want* this!'

She hunched low, swaying from side to side, as Annabelle prepared to serve again. Five bounces and the big kicking topspin to Roxy's forehand followed. Roxy was waiting for it and slapped a hard flat return straight down the line for a winner.

Match point. Roxy wasted no time in launching her body into her own serve. The power forced Annabelle back beyond the baseline from where she could only muster a tame return. Watching the ball come back to her, Roxy pretended she was going to go for the big cross-court winner, but at the last moment, she changed her body shape and softly dinked a drop-shot just over the net.

Annabelle immediately sprinted forward, reaching the ball just in time to fire her own backhand down-the-line pass beyond Roxy who was stranded midcourt. Roxy turned and raced after the ball. Catching up with it, she extended her arm as far it would go, bringing her forehand back up, around and over the ball at such speed that it spun into the air, laced with deadly topspin.

Straining every muscle, Roxy emitted an animal noise unlike any she had ever made before.

'Arrrgghhh!' she growled, as the lob flew up from her racket.

The ball arced high into the air, looping over Annabelle and her attempts to reach it, before dipping back down in time to bounce just within the baseline. The perfect topspin lob. Unstoppable.

'Game, set, match,' announced the umpire, barely audible above Roxy's thunderous roar of celebration. 'Roxana Campbell wins two sets to one: 6–4, 1–6, 7–6. She now goes on to represent the county in the National Finals at Wimbledon.'

Suddenly, all of Roxy's thoughts became jumbled up. She felt so dizzy and her body had become unbearably heavy. As she crumpled to the ground, she could hear her dad running onto the court towards her.

'Amazing, Roxy!' he yelled, scooping her up into his arms. 'You did it! YOU! You're going to Wimbledon!'

'Dad . . .' she whispered. 'It feels . . . so . . . good . . .' Her eyes shut. In the distance, just before she lost consciousness, she could dimly hear Daryll screaming: 'Help! WE NEED HELP!'

PART 3
COME BACK

TWO WEEKS LATER

SUNDAY
24th JUNE

Kaine looked at Roxy as she lay, motionless, in her hospital bed. Only the beeps of the machine that monitored her heart rate proved that she was still alive.

It had been ten days since the bandages had been removed from her bald skull. The track of black stitches ran from the top of her head, where they had cut her open, all the way across to her ear.

He closed his eyes and, as always, the series of events started replaying in his mind ... He had just got home and was giving his mum a hug and apologizing for making her worry when his dad had called ... Something had happened to Roxy, he didn't know what it was, but it was serious ... The piercing sound of his mum's shriek . . . her repeating over and over: 'Not again. This can't be happening again!'

When the doctor had finally explained that Roxy was in a coma because a blood vessel had burst in her head and lots of blood had got into her brain, his mum and dad had both started crying.

'She told me she was having headaches,' Samantha had said, tears streaming down her cheeks. 'I should have known she wouldn't have complained unless it was something serious.'

Kaine had not yet cried himself. Even when they were told that Roxy might not ever wake up, he had still not broken down. Everything inside him was blocked, and he did not know how to let it out.

He felt his phone vibrate. There was a new message. His heart pumped hard and fast as he read its words:

> V sorry to hear about what happened to your sister.
> I have left you be as I understand that this is a difficult time.
> Please contact me when you can.
> I need you to do a job for me.
> SS

Kaine instantly turned his phone off and put it back in his tracksuit trousers as though the act of removing it from his sight might take away the information that he had just seen. He could not deal with the thought of Sheldon right now. It was one problem too many.

The door to Roxy's room opened and in walked Malin, the nurse who looked after her most of the time. As she took Roxy's blood pressure and made some notes, she looked at Kaine.

'Still no luck?' she asked.

Kaine shook his head. The doctors and Malin had all suggested that it would be a good idea for the family to talk to Roxy, and his mum and dad did it all the time, but Kaine had not yet managed to utter a single word to her.

Malin sat down next to Kaine and took his hand. With thick red hair and skin so pale she looked almost like a doll, she was a very beautiful woman. Kaine found it difficult to look her in the eye.

'You know,' she said. 'It's not just for Roxy. We think if you talked to her, it'd be good for you too.'

Kaine didn't react. He could hear the clock in the room ticking.

'How close are you two?' asked Malin softly.

Kaine shook his head. He dreamed about Roxy every night. 'We used to be . . .' he said slowly. 'When we were younger, we weren't just twins . . . we were best friends. We did everything together, supported each other . . . especially with our sport. I was going to play in the Premier League and she was going to win Wimbledon. That was our dream and we used to say that, when one of us wasn't playing, the other one could take all the power, use it for their game . . .'

'Sweet,' said Malin. 'And then?'

'I don't know,' said Kaine. 'I think it changed when we went to secondary school. We . . . just weren't as close and . . . I said some horrible things . . . That's why I can't talk to her now. I feel . . . so bad . . .'

He buried his head in his hands. He constantly thought about how mean he had been to her at school and yet, despite it all, Roxy had still asked AJ to make sure he was safe that day when Ellis Small could have killed him. She had saved him.

'Look,' said Malin, showing Kaine her two fists. 'This,' she said shaking her left fist, 'is your past.' She made a gesture as if to throw it away. 'It's gone. Forget it. This,' she said shaking her right fist, which she then opened, 'is your future. You can still write it. Talk to her, Kaine, talk to her about anything. It doesn't matter. Just talk to her, and tell her how you feel.'

She rubbed Kaine's arm and then left the room.

Kaine looked at Roxy again. He opened his mouth . . . tried to talk, but nothing came out.

5 DAYS LATER

FRIDAY
29TH JUNE

In the three weeks since the accident, the Campbell family's entire existence had been based around being with Roxy. They arranged their lives so that at least one of them was with her every day. If and when she woke up, they wanted to be there for her.

Today, however, Kaine, Samantha and Daryll had to be somewhere else before they could go to see Roxy. It was 7.45 a.m. and they were sitting in the Principal's office at Compton Academy. It felt strange to Kaine to be anywhere other than the flat or the hospital.

'Firstly,' said Mrs Buckland, 'I want to say how devastated we are about Roxy. We desperately hope she pulls though. We miss her terribly and we just can't imagine what you are all going through.'

Kaine looked at his mum and dad. They both seemed like they had aged twenty years in the last 19 days. He knew that even in the times that they weren't with Roxy physically, they were with her mentally all day, every day.

'Now, as regards Kaine,' continued Mrs Buckland. 'In setting off the fire alarm, we can all agree he did a monumentally stupid thing. And, as you know, at the time it happened, my intention was to exclude him from the school. However . . . with everything that's happened, I want to support you in any way that we possibly can . . . so Mr Kerrigan and I have a proposal for you. We will have Kaine back in school—'

'Thank you,' said Samantha, grabbing Kaine's hand. 'He'll behave this time. He's promised me, haven't you?'

'Yes, Mrs Buckland,' Kaine said.

'That's good to hear . . . but our offer comes with a condition . . . To make sure we can trust Kaine, Daryll – we would need you also to spend some time in and around school . . . partly to keep an eye on Kaine . . . but we would also give you some other responsibilities.'

'Sorry, I'm not sure what you mean.' said Daryll, looking confused.

'We were trying to work out how we could find a

solution with Kaine,' said Mr Kerrigan. 'And the idea occurred to us that we might be able to find a solution that works for all parties. You see, I could also do with an extra pair of hands in the PE department . . .'

'Are you saying I should work in the school?' asked Daryll.

'Yes,' said Mr Kerrigan. 'Like I said, we think it could be a good idea . . . for everyone.'

'The thing is,' said Daryll, shaking his head, 'I'm just not cut out for being in a school. Never have been.'

'The plan would be that you would be here on a part-time basis,' continued Mrs Buckland calmly. 'To make sure that Kaine was behaving, and also assist Mr Kerrigan in the PE department . . . We can only accept Kaine back under supervision and we felt you might be the best person to do this.'

'It would just be on a trial arrangement at first,' said Mr Kerrigan. 'You've already got your DBS from using the school court with Roxy, so we could get going quite quickly. See how it works for all of us. And we would, of course, pay you for your time . . .'

Daryll was about to argue again and Kaine also wanted to say that there was no way he wanted his dad in school, but the way that Mrs Buckland and his mum were nodding to each other told him that the decision had already been taken. Kaine was to start back at school on Monday morning, and his dad would be joining him.

While his parents went through some of the paper-work with Mrs Buckland, Mr Kerrigan and Kaine were walking together through the empty hallways of Compton Academy. None of the other kids were in yet. It was the earliest Kaine had ever been in school.

'How are you all doing?' asked Mr Kerrigan.

'It's like it's not real,' said Kaine. 'Being back here . . . It's strange because it feels like it was just a nightmare. Like it all happened to someone else. I can't . . . believe that it's Roxy.'

They walked in silence for a little while.

'Sir,' said Kaine as they arrived at the big assembly hall. The caretakers were putting all the chairs out. 'With everything that's happened . . . to Roxy . . . I haven't seen you . . . to thank you properly for what you did . . . for me.'

The memories of that day haunted Kaine. If he touched his neck, he could still feel the bruises where Ellis Small had almost strangled him to death.

Mr Kerrigan stopped walking and looked at Kaine. 'Come with me,' he said. 'I need to talk to you.'

They walked into the cafeteria and Mr Kerrigan got himself a cup of coffee from the drinks machine. Then they sat down at one of the dinner tables.

'Kaine,' he said. 'I know your head must be all over the place, but I just have to say this to you again. People like Ellis Small and Sheldon Statham – if you get involved in their world, if you become part of it, it only ends up in one of two ways: death or prison. That's it. Those are the only two choices.'

Kaine looked down at the floor.

'How did you get mixed up in all this, Kaine?'

'I don't even know,' said Kaine. 'Some of it started when me and Rufus got into an argument playing football and I said something stupid . . . about his mum – and it just kind of just grew from there . . .'

'It's frightening,' said Mr Kerrigan. 'One little argument . . . just the smallest thing. That's all it takes.'

'I think I'm calm,' said Kaine. 'And then one person says one thing and I'm gone; it's like a fire in my head and I can't think straight. I just want to fight and destroy them.' His fist was clenched and he pressed it down hard on the table.

'I know that feeling,' said Mr Kerrigan. 'I know that fire . . . Well, hopefully having your dad around will help a bit on that front. I'm also going to suggest that you having a curfew would be a good idea. If you're not at the hospital, I think you should be at home before it gets dark.'

'I don't want my dad here,' said Kaine, shaking his head. 'He winds me up more than anyone. And now it's going to be even worse. Does he have to come to school?'

'We need to make sure you stay out of trouble, Kaine. And we have to keep you safe too. You didn't want the police involved in what happened with Ellis Small. That was your decision. And we didn't tell your parents either. But that doesn't mean it's all gone away. You know what's happening around the area. We've got to be careful. I can't always be with you the whole time. We need someone who cares.'

'Dad doesn't care about me,' said Kaine. 'He only cares about Roxy.'

Just saying her name and thinking about her lying in hospital, made Kaine feel as though someone had punched him right in the stomach.

'That can't be true,' said Mr Kerrigan, setting down his drink and scrunching Kaine's shoulder. 'I mean, I know you have your ups and downs, but he must be proud of you. Especially your football.'

Kaine stared at his shoes. He didn't want to answer, but he could feel Mr Kerrigan was still watching him, waiting until he did:

'My dad's never said he's proud of me in my life.'

SUNDAY
1st JULY

Kaine sat in his room and sent AJ a message to let him know he'd be back at school on Monday. Almost immediately his phone beeped back. But it wasn't AJ.

> Do not ignore me, Kaine.
> I expect you to come and see me in the next 48 hours.
> SS

Kaine's heart was beating in his throat. He tried to compose a response, telling Sheldon to leave him alone. But it was no use. It was impossible to tell Sheldon what to do, especially after Kaine had promised him that he was in for good. He put his phone away and went into

Roxy's room. He still hadn't cried, and he still hadn't been able to talk to her. He wondered if there was something wrong with him. If there was a bit of him missing or if, perhaps, after what had happened with Mamma, his emotions had gone numb.

He started looking around her room for her diary. She took that diary everywhere with her and guarded it with her life. Kaine thought that if he could find it, and if he could read it and hear her thoughts, then it might unlock something. A thought, a memory . . . just something to bring him back from the dead feeling he had inside.

The diary wasn't in the drawers of her desk. Or her cupboard. He searched her sports bag. No joy. He tried to tune into the connection they had that sometimes allowed them to sense each other's thoughts, but it was no use. He collapsed onto her bed in frustration and, as he did so, he felt something hard underneath. He got up and lifted up the mattress. And there it was.

He retrieved the diary and looked at it. He took a deep breath and opened it somewhere near the middle. He flicked through a few of the pages until a set of words immediately made him start reading:

. . . I have a confession to make. I cut Kaine's boots yesterday. I don't even know why I did it. I just feel like ~~I'm a~~ I'm stressed the whole time and he goes around doing whatever he wants, saying whatever he wants, and . . . I just want him to feel a bit of what I feel every day.

Kaine stared at the words. For a second he was still. Then he felt the rage erupt within him. He sprinted out of the front door, down the steps, and ran all the way to the hospital. As soon as he got there, he took the lift up to the eighth floor and stormed into Roxy's room.

'Why did you do it, Roxy?' he yelled. 'I know what you did to my boots! . . . Why?!'

Part of him expected her to sit up and shout back at him to defend herself, just like she always did. But there was nothing. Just the beeps of her heart monitor.

'Tell me, Roxy,' he shouted. 'I want to know right now! Why would you want to do that? You knew football was all I had. Why did you have to ruin it? What's wrong with you, Roxy?'

He punched the wall and slumped down into a chair. Although he was still breathing hard and his heart was still thumping, the rage inside him was not quite so strong now. He wondered whether shouting at Roxy counted as talking to her.

'I heard some noise – are you OK, love?' Malin asked.

Kaine had been so lost in his thoughts he hadn't heard her come in. He didn't answer.

'Well, I'll just be on the Heathcoat Ward next door if you need me,' she said.

When she left, Kaine remained sitting in the chair for a very long time. Then, finally, he got up and moved his chair to sit down by Roxy, resting his head on her stomach. He held her hand and lifted it up to place it against his cheek. He could feel her pulse beating. It was so weak he was scared it might stop at any moment. He felt a teardrop fall from his eye onto her bed.

'I'm . . . sorry, Roxy,' he whispered. 'Sorry for all the horrible things I've said to you. You were right to do what you did to the boots. I deserved it. For the way I've been the last few months. I just . . . felt angry . . . all the time . . . About Dad, about you, about Mamma . . . I did blame you. All of you. I admit it. I know it wasn't your fault. But I wanted it to be. So I could have someone to be angry at. Feeling the anger was . . . easier than feeling the pain. And the guilt. I don't know why I panicked so much. I should have known what to do.

I should have saved her. She would still be here now. I won't ever let it happen again. I'll never panic like that again. If you ever come back . . . and you need me, I'll be there. I promise I will. But you can't go now, Roxy. You can't leave . . .'

Suddenly, he felt himself drowning in a sea of sadness.

'Just come back now, Roxy . . . I promise everything will be better . . .'

He let his sister's hand feel the stream of tears that were running down his cheek. 'Just come back now, OK?'

MONDAY
2nd JULY

It was break time, and Kaine was still trying to get used to being back at school. It felt completely wrong not to have Roxy there. Meanwhile, it was beyond embarrassing to have his dad there too, walking around like an idiot in his PE outfit. Kaine was sitting quietly with AJ and Queenie having a baguette when Daryll strode up to him in front of everyone.

'Mr Kerrigan just told me that you're not playing football any more. What's all that about?' he said.

'I don't want to talk about it,' Kaine said, cringing as everyone turned to look at them talking. 'And I told you, please don't try to talk to me in school.'

Kaine saw his dad's face drop. 'Can I talk to you in private, then?' he asked.

'I'm busy,' said Kaine.

'It'll just take a secon—'

'I'll speak to you later, all right?' said Kaine. He got up and walked away. His dad had only been in school a couple of hours and he was already pressurizing him. Now he knew how Roxy must have felt for the last few months.

When he got home from school that night, Kaine went to his room and listened to some music. He thought about how he had felt when he was speaking to Roxy for the first time. Even though she hadn't been able to talk back to him, he had sensed she was *there*, listening to him. He wanted to try to save her like she had saved him from Ellis. He had decided that he would now talk to her whenever he went to see her and, one day, when she woke up, they would go back to how they had been when they were younger: best friends, inseparable, a team.

He heard his mum moving around in the kitchen and knew that now was the time to tell her. He could not put it off any more. He was scared of what was going to happen when she found out, but he had no choice. He was in trouble, and he couldn't see a way out.

'Mum,' he said nervously, as he walked into the kitchen. 'I need to talk to you about something. It's important.'

He watched his mum, who was cleaning the surface by the sink even though it wasn't dirty.

'What is it?' she said.

He didn't reply straightaway.

She stopped and turned to look at him. 'What is it, Kaine?' she repeated. 'I haven't got the energy to play games.'

'I did some stupid things,' he said. He could feel his stomach churning as though he was about to be sick.

'What stupid things?'

'I . . . got involved with people that I shouldn't have . . . and Sheldon Statham keeps texting me.'

'Sheldon Statham?! What does Sheldon Statham want with you?'

'I . . . before everything happened with Roxy . . . I started doing some things for him . . . I've stopped now, but he keeps texting me.'

'Sheldon Statham?!' Samantha repeated again. Kaine could see the look of disgust on her face. 'After everything our family has been through? You get involved with someone like him? Are you that brainless? He runs gangs, Kaine! That's what he does! That's how boys get themselves killed!'

'I know! I *know*! I've stopped . . . I promise you I've stopped. But . . . he won't let me.'

'What do you mean, Kaine? What are you trying to tell me?'

'He's hassling me . . . He won't leave me alone. I'm . . . scared, Mum.'

Samantha sat down at the kitchen table and held her head in her hands. 'First Roxy,' she said. 'Now this?'

'I'm sorry,' Kaine said. 'I didn't want to worry you. But . . . I just don't know what to do.'

'Have you got these texts on your phone?'

Kaine nodded.

'Fine. We'll go to the police. This is harassment. He can't do that.'

Kaine shook his head. 'We *can't* do that. He knows everything. If we snitch on him, he'll . . .'

He watched his mum close her eyes and try not to cry.

'I'm sorry,' he said again.

'You need to tell me the complete truth, Kaine,' she said. 'Right now. I need to know everything. You said you did "things" for him. What exactly did you do for that . . . man? Did he make you move drugs? Have you got any weapons?'

'No,' said Kaine, shuddering as he remembered putting the knife into the rubbish bin at Sheldon's empty flat. 'I just did little jobs . . . passing on messages . . . I realized it was wrong pretty much as soon as I started, but it was already . . . too late.'

'Of course it's too late. How many times have we discussed this, Kaine? It's too late the minute he gets his claws into you. And what did he give you in return for these jobs?'

'Money.'

'How much?'

'I don't know.'

'What do you mean you don't know? How much?'

'Maybe about two hundred pounds.'

'Two hundred pounds?!'

'And, when I ran away, I stayed at his place.'

'You did what?' said Samantha, her eyes burning with fire. 'If he laid one finger on you—'

'No, it wasn't like that. He wasn't even there. But . . . I promised him I was in for good. And he's bought me some meals and stuff too. That's why he's not letting me go.'

Samantha shook her head and looked at him.

'Tell me what to do,' he said. 'Please, just tell me what to do and I'll do it.'

'I'll tell you what we're going to do,' she said. 'You're going to text him right now and tell him that you are never going to see him again but that I will give him back his two hundred pounds and that that will be the end of the matter. And, once you've done that, you just leave it to me. You block him from your phone, and if he ever comes and tries to see you or talk to, you tell me straightaway. OK?'

'I swear,' he said.

'I don't even know where I'm going to get the money from,' she said. 'But I'll find it. If it'll put an end to all this, I'll find it. Go on. I want to see you send that text right now.'

Kaine got out his phone and typed in the message:

> Please stop contacting me Sheldon.
> I've told my mum everything.
> She's going to pay you back the
> money you gave me.
> Kaine

He showed his mum and pressed send. Then he blocked Sheldon's number.

'Good,' she said. She looked at him for a long time. Then she said: 'Now I want you to come and give me a hug.'

Kaine walked towards his mum and wrapped his arms around her.

'If I know what's happening, then I can help you,' she said.

'I didn't want to worry you,' said Kaine. 'With Roxy . . .'

'The only time you worry me is when you go quiet on me. Promise me you'll always talk to me.'

'I will . . . but what if Sheldon won't let me go?'

'I told you to leave that to me.'

Kaine nodded and buried his head in his mum's hug. He felt like he was a young boy again. It felt good.

TUESDAY
3rd JULY

Samantha got back from the hospital the next day and slumped down into the chair by the kitchen table. It was covered with the countless unpaid bills she had taken out and spread on the surface before going to visit Roxy. She stared at all the letters, notices and final warnings before picking up the calculator and starting to tap in the numbers. No matter which way she put them in, there was no way she could make them work. All the time spent at the hospital had meant that she hadn't been able to do as many shifts as she'd needed to.

She leaned back and looked up at the ceiling. Even if Daryll was given the job full-time at school, she knew it still wouldn't be enough. The bills had piled up too high. And now there was Kaine's debt to settle too.

She shook her head and walked slowly into her bedroom. Opening her clothes cupboard, she reached into the bottom drawer and pulled out the black box. Her mum's black box. She unlocked it, and moving aside the reams of notes, papers and photographs, she clasped the little velvet ring case.

She sat on the bed, opened up the case and looked at her mother's wedding ring. Even in an unlit room it still shone brightly. Feeling a mixture of sadness and guilt, she was just about to lock the box and take the ring down to the jewellery shop to sell it when something caught her eye. It was a big, thick envelope with the word *Anthony* written on it. She instinctively knew that inside would be all the papers and notes her mum had kept relating to Anthony's murder. Just seeing the file sent her mind spinning back.

She had been so young, but she could still remember her mum calling the police on a daily basis to ask why they hadn't found the killer and brought him to justice. She could recall her mum asking her whenever they saw a boy who looked the right age, whether that was him, whether he was the one who had stabbed Anthony.

But it had always made Samantha cry, so her mum

stopped asking her the question. Samantha had felt so guilty that she had not been able to find the boy, and she could vividly remember the vow she had made to her mother when she was only nine years old. 'I will find him, Mum,' she had said. 'I promise you, one day I will find him.'

PART 4
NEVER ORDINARY

ONE WEEK LATER

TUESDAY
10th JULY

'Hi, Roxy, Kaine here again. I'm really sorry I haven't been to see you the last couple of days. I told Mum that I had got myself involved with Sheldon Statham, and she's been insisting that I pretty much don't go anywhere by myself. She's even downstairs now, waiting to take me home. Her and Dad are also being seriously strict about me always being home before it gets dark too. I don't mind. I understand that they want me to be safe.

'Anyway, I was thinking about you even more these last couple of days, and I've decided something. You know how I've started talking to you when I come and see you? Well, you better get used to it because I've decided that I'm going to do it even more. I'm going to talk to you so much – and tell you every single thing that is happening – that in the end you're going to get so bored with hearing my voice that you're going to have to wake up, just to shut me up.'

He looked at her, trying to remember what her smile looked like. Her real, true, happy smile.

'OK, so here goes . . . Well, for a start, you know it's nearly the summer holidays? Only eight days left of school. Can you believe it? I don't know what Mum and Dad will say about me hanging around on the estate in the holidays. It's definitely getting more dangerous. You can feel it. Sheldon and Ellis Small from Park Avenue are properly at war now and it's scary. There's been quite a few stabbings and it's getting worse. They've got a policeman outside school most of the time at the moment too. Sometimes, school actually feels like the safest place to be.

'Talking of school, Dad's now started doing some of the football coaching. AJ says he's actually really good. I can't believe it – you know what Dad's like – but AJ swears he's quality. Everyone at school calls him K2 because they reckon with his shaved head and his tracksuit, he's like another Mr K. Rebooted. He's asked me to play a few times, but I've told him I'm not playing football . . . Don't worry, it's not cos I don't have any boots . . . I just . . . don't want to.

'By the way, at home he's started to do weird things, like he makes dinner for me and Mum quite a lot now and . . . I'm not one hundred per cent sure about this . . . but I think he might have stopped drinking. Oh – and this is the really disgusting bit – but . . . him and Mum have started hugging the whole time, like before, when we were younger. Remember how we used to pull them apart and tell them that it was gross? Well, it's like that. If they're ever at home at the same time, they sit and watch TV together holding hands and sometimes they kiss . . . makes me want to puke! Roxy . . . ? It looked like you smiled there . . .

'Anyway, speaking of *kissing*, you know AJ came to see you yesterday? He asks about you every day in school too. I don't know why he likes you so much. I told him you're not that great, but he doesn't seem to listen. Oh, by the way, we don't hang around with Jasmine and Tochi any more. The way they were with you . . . wasn't cool. I know the way I was with you wasn't cool either. I had no idea that I hurt you so much when I was mean to you, Roxy. I read it in your diary – how it made you feel – and I'm so sorry for saying all those things. I honestly didn't think they upset you that much.

'And I'm sorry for reading your diary too. Please don't get mad at me. I know it's private and I know it's secret, but I can't help it. I read a page every night. It's like you're back and you're talking to me. That's what I need, Roxy. I need you back . . . I need you to talk to me.'

FRIDAY
13th JULY

Kaine and AJ were in the library for a private study lesson, but they weren't doing any work.

'You gonna play against Patchmore?' asked AJ. 'Last match of the whole year.'

Kaine shook his head.

'Come on, Kaine,' he said. 'We need you, man. Why not? Are you still upset about the scout?'

'It's not that,' Kaine said. He put down his pen and looked at his friend. 'I need to get out of here,' he said. 'Tell miss I've gone to the toilet.'

When the librarian left her desk, Kaine quickly sneaked out through the door. He didn't know where he was going, but he just needed some fresh air. After a couple of minutes he saw that his feet had taken him towards the school playing fields. On the far-side pitch, his dad was taking a football session for the Year 7s. Kaine walked towards it and then stopped and stood behind a tree to stay out of sight.

'That's brilliant, Stevie Marshall,' he could hear his dad calling from the sidelines. 'What you did there is perfect. The way you tucked back in when the left back went forward, that's total football. Love it!'

Kaine poked his head around the tree just to double-check that it was actually the same dad that he had grown up with.

'What are you doing hiding there?' his dad called out, catching sight of Kaine.

'I . . . erm . . . needed the shade . . .' said Kaine.

'Right . . .' said Daryll, coming over to him. 'Well, since you're here, do you fancy making up the numbers? We're one short.'

Kaine looked out onto the pitch. The boys were chasing after the ball. The lush green grass looked perfect. He could feel his feet start to tingle. 'No thanks,' he said.

'Ah, come on,' said Daryll. 'Just ten minutes. What harm can it do? We need someone to fill in in midfield.

'I don't have boots. And, anyway, I'm— I was a striker.'

'I know,' said Daryll, looking at Kaine. 'But I was reading this book about Barcelona at the hospital last night. Did you know that when Guardiola was their manager, one of the ways he got the best out of Messi was to play him a bit deeper?'

Kaine almost choked. He didn't know what was more ridiculous: the idea of him playing in midfield or the fact that his dad had actually been reading a book.

'I started thinking about you,' said Daryll. 'With all your power and acceleration, you could run the game from the midfield . . . I can imagine you prowling around the pitch like a—'

'Lion?'

'Exactly!' said Daryll. 'That's exactly what you'd be like. How did you know that's what I was going to say?'

'Just a guess,' said Kaine.

'So what do you say, Kaine? We've got some spare boots. Come and have a knockabout in midfield. You'll enjoy it. And . . . I promise you, I won't criticize you once. You're too good not to play football, Kaine.'

Kaine looked at the ground. He wondered whether that was the nicest thing his dad had ever said to him.

'Come on, Kaine,' said Daryll. 'Football makes you happy, and God knows, we all need something to keep us going right now.'

Kaine stared at the goal closest to him. He imagined curling one right into the top corner. Again the tingling feeling returned.

'Sorry,' he said, forcing himself to walk away. 'I just . . . can't.'

SUNDAY
15th JULY

Kaine lay on Roxy's bed, switched on her lamp, and took out her diary. He was almost at the end now.

I just wish I could disappear and no one could ever find me again. And, you know what? If I did, no one would even miss me.

He closed his eyes and shook his head. He'd had no idea that Roxy had felt so alone. Then he heard something drop out of the diary and onto the carpet. He leaned down and picked it up.

It was the old family photo that Roxy had tried to show him that day by the garages. The one from when they were just kids. The one that he had thrown in the rubbish bin. She must have taken it back out and kept it. He looked at the seven-year-old versions of themselves doing a high-five in the photo. He thought to himself that it was strange that it was the little things that he missed most. He wished he could do a high-five with Roxy now. They always seemed to get the absolute perfect timing.

'Kaine?' said his dad, walking in. 'I've been looking for you. What are you doing in here?'

'Sometimes . . . it just . . . helps,' said Kaine. 'I think.'

'Well,' said Daryll. 'Maybe . . . I'm hoping . . . this might help a bit too. Fancy trying them out against Patchmore on Wednesday?' He was opening a box to reveal a set of brand-new, gold-coloured football boots. 'It should never have taken me so long,' he said. 'But . . . Happy Birthday.'

'You shouldn't have got these,' said Kaine, unable to take his eyes off the gleaming boots. 'I know how much they cost.'

'It's OK,' said Daryll. 'I'm earning it and Mr Kerrigan told me on Friday that they're going to take me on permanently, on a full-time basis. We're good for it.'

'Congratulations,' said Kaine. He couldn't stop

staring at the boots. He thought they were probably the most beautiful things he had ever seen in his life. But he didn't take hold of the box. 'I appreciate it,' he said. 'But, like I told you, I don't want to play.'

Kaine saw an expression of such sadness on his dad's face.

'It's me, isn't it?' said Daryll, sitting down next to him on the bed. 'I know I made so many mistakes with you . . . and with Roxy too . . . Nothing I can ever do will fix that . . . but I'm learning and . . . I'm trying and I would hate myself if I thought I'd put you off football for ever . . . Look, just keep the boots. I want you to have them. It's not about you playing in the match . . . It's about . . . I just . . . wanted to give you your birthday present.'

Kaine watched Daryll walk slowly out of the room. When he was by himself, he picked up the boots and held them in his hands. He could feel his eyes start to water and his feet start to tingle. They were tingling so much he had to listen to them. He put the boots on and laced them up. Then he picked up one of Roxy's tennis balls and slid out of her window and down the fire escape.

Twenty minutes later, Kaine crawled back in through

the window and picked up one of Roxy's pens. He opened her diary to a new page and began writing:

Roxy, I hope one day you get to read this
I m not good at writing like you ~~are~~ but I ve just read the last page of your diary
I don't know what to say
I m so sorry that you were so unhappy
I swear I didn't know
I thought *you* were happy and I was the only one that was unhappy
I think I felt alone too   How stupid is it that we were both feeling alone when we were always both right there?
I want you to know Roxy that ~~I love~~ I love you, we all love you
I've just been ~~kik~~ kicking a tennis ball around
Its the   first time I've kicked a ball in weeks
AJ thinks I haven t been playing because of the scout, Dad thinks I m ~~bec~~ not playing because of him and the way he used to shout at me when I played but its not because of either of those things
Its because I didn t think it was ~~rigt~~ right Roxy
How can I go out and play when you re like you are?
I know you would give anything to be out there playing so

how can ~~I~~ play and not ~~this~~ think of you? I just thought
I would feel too guilty

You're the one that should be playing and I should
be the one in your ~~pos~~ position you saved me Roxy I'll
never forget that

Dad just gave me some ~~tr~~ new boots for my birthday
present and my feet were tingling so much that I just
had to go out and try them out

It felt amazing Roxy you know that feeling when
the ball does what you ~~want~~ want like its your friend?

Theres a game on Wednesday Roxy the last match of the
season

And I think I want to play but I want to know if its
OK with you? Is it all right Roxy? Remember how we
~~used~~ used to give each other our power? Will you give me
your power Roxy? If I feel like I have ~~your~~ your
power with me I know I can do anything

And, if I play, I promise I'll think about you every
minute of the match and I'll try so hard to make you proud

Kaine

WEDNESDAY
18th JULY

Under-14s Match
Compton Academy v Patchmore School

Kaine crunched into the tackle, winning the ball back for Compton before playing it out to the wing and sprinting into the box.

'Beautiful, Kaine!' Daryll shouted from the sidelines.

Kaine drove himself forward. He believed he had the strength of two people within him. Every step he took, every run he made, it felt as though he had all of Roxy's energy and talent inside him too.

Kaine surged into the box and, seeing a cross coming back in towards him, he leaped high into the air, softly guiding the ball back for AJ, who was waiting, perfectly positioned by the penalty spot. The pass was like a gift-wrapped present and AJ smashed it, first time, into the roof of the net. Seeing the ball go in, AJ jumped into the air to celebrate, and Kaine was the first person to join him.

Compton won 4–0, and at the end of the game, Kaine went to shake the hand of all the Patchmore players. He knew how lucky he was to be out there. He knew how lucky they all were to be playing the game they loved.

As he came off the pitch, he pointed to his boots and gave his dad the thumbs up. Daryll smiled and said one word: 'Beautiful.'

'Welcome back,' said AJ, running over to give Kaine a fistbump. 'That's the best I've ever seen you play.'

'Thanks,' said Kaine. 'I felt like I was playing for Roxy.'

AJ put his arm around Kaine and they walked off the pitch together, reliving every moment of the game. Kaine was so engrossed in the conversation that he failed to notice the man walking straight towards him.

'Hello again, Kaine,' said the man.

'Hi,' said Kaine, immediately recognizing Brian, the Southampton scout. 'I . . . didn't think I'd be seeing you again.'

Within twenty minutes, Kaine was sprinting down the hospital corridor so fast he almost sent Malin flying.

'Someone's in a rush,' she said.

'Sorry, Malin,' he shouted over his shoulder. 'Got something I need to tell Roxy!'

He burst into his sister's room and shouted: 'Roxy!! You are not going to believe what just happened!' He pushed the chair out of the way and knelt down on the floor beside her. 'Southampton have asked me to go for a trial! The scout came to see me play again today and I had one of my best games ever! He wants me to go and play in a match at their training ground in front of the Academy Director! This is it, Roxy . . . It's actually happening!'

There was no response. Just the beeps of the heart monitor. Kaine looked at Roxy. Her face was so peaceful she almost seemed to look happy.

'You know, it felt like it wasn't just me playing out there today. It really felt like it was both of us. I swear that's why no one could stop me. Thank you, Roxy . . . you made my dream come true . . . Give me a high-five . . .'

Kaine held out his hand and smiled. Then his heart stopped.

Roxy's hand seemed to be twitching. Then, very slowly, it started to raise itself upwards.

'Ro . . .' said Kaine. 'Are you . . .'

He moved his hand towards hers and, as they made contact, he saw her eyelids start to flicker.

'Roxy!' Kaine cried. 'Roxy! Wait there!'

He ran like lightning into the corridor.

'Malin!!' he yelled at the top of his voice. 'Malin! Please come quick!!'

Half an hour later, the doctors reopened the door and Kaine and his parents hurried into the room. Roxy was sitting up, with her eyes open.

'Hey,' she said softly.

'My baby!' Samantha cried, running towards Roxy, covering her with kisses. 'My poor baby. I thought . . . I can't believe it!'

'Hi, Mum,' said Roxy, kissing Samantha back. She looked weak and a little confused. Then she saw Kaine. 'Hey, Bro,' she said, through her tears. She held out her hand.

Kaine started half weeping, half laughing. Happiness and relief rushed through him like an overflowing river. 'Hey, Sis,' he said, walking over and taking her hand in his.

'How are you?' she asked.

'I'm OK,' he said, swallowing his tears. 'Now . . . you're . . . here. How do you feel?'

Roxy smiled. Kaine could see some of her old self returning. 'It's strange,' she said. 'The only way I can . . . describe it is that I felt as though I was in a dream for such a long time and . . . in the dream I was covered and surrounded and locked in by loads of pillows. They were all over me. I was trying to move them . . . trying to get them off me . . . to get out . . . but they were all around me and I couldn't do it. Until now . . .'

Kaine hugged her tightly. He never wanted to let her go again.

'Dad,' said Roxy, reaching out her hand to Daryll. 'What . . . happened?'

'You've been in a coma, Roxy,' said Daryll. 'I thought the doctors told you.'

'No,' she said. 'The Finals. Did I win?'

'Yes,' said Daryll. 'Of course you won. You were absolutely incredible, Roxy . . . I can't believe that's the first thing you ask after you've been unconscious for over five weeks!'

'I thought so,' said Roxy. 'Just wanted to make sure. That game . . . it was special. It made me realize how much I love it. I just want to make up for all the time we've lost.'

Roxy and Daryll both smiled. Then, as Roxy reached down to her thigh, a sudden look of panic haunted her face.

'Dad,' she cried. 'Dad, what's happening? I can't . . . I can't feel my legs!'

THURSDAY
19th JULY

Twenty-four hours later, Samantha and Daryll were called to a meeting with Mr Rothman, the surgeon who had been treating Roxy.

'This morning,' he said, 'we conducted a second operation on Roxy. It was a nine-hour procedure on her back. We found an abnormality in her spinal chord. That's what caused the bleeding on the brain.'

Samantha tried to take in the severity of what they were being told. Another nine-hour operation. After everything Roxy had already been through.

'And this . . . abnormality,' said Daryll. 'That's why Roxy couldn't feel her legs?'

'Yes,' said the doctor. 'We had hoped that the

operation might give her back some use of her legs, but . . . I'm afraid, despite all our efforts – and believe me, we tried everything – we couldn't achieve that. I'm very sorry.'

'What does it mean?' asked Daryll. 'Is it . . . do you think she'll be able to play tennis again?'

The doctor shook his head. 'I'm so very sorry,' he said. 'As I say, we tried absolutely everything we could, but it's not something that we are able to reverse. Roxy will not be able to move her legs.'

Samantha felt Daryll's body starting to slump. She could feel his colossal frame falling into her.

'But . . .' said Daryll. 'There must be something. All these medical advances, everything we see on the news. Surely. This girl is a *fighter*, Doctor. You don't know what she's capable of.'

The doctor shook his head once more. 'I realize what a terrible blow this is – and we will be making counsellors available to Roxy and the family to help you through this time . . . but you should be comforted by the fact that people with physical disabilities are able to lead full and normal—'

The doctor was still talking, but Samantha could see that Daryll couldn't hear him. Through her own tears, she hugged Daryll and said: 'It's all right. It's going to be OK.'

Daryll was crying now. 'Not my Roxy!' he wept. 'Not my Roxy!'

Samantha hugged him as tightly as she could, using all her strength to stop him from collapsing.

Much later, Roxy was alone, lying in her bed.

When Mr Rothman had told her the diagnosis, she had heard what the surgeon said, but the information had not gone in. She couldn't equate what he was saying with her own life. It was as though she was watching a programme on TV about someone else.

She looked out of the window into the darkening sky. The holidays were just starting. Some people would be going to the cinema, maybe kissing in the back row, some people would going out to a party . . . She wondered what AJ was doing right now. She shook her head. She would not allow herself to feel self-pity. She craned her neck to check that none of the nurses were around and then she pushed herself upright in her bed.

She looked at her right arm. Her serving arm. After five weeks of not being used, her biceps had all but disappeared. The flesh all over her body was thin and saggy with no muscles left at all. She thought back to that last day at the tournament, to how strong and determined she had been. How could that person now be expected to spend the rest of her life in a wheelchair?

The images of her playing tennis, chasing down balls and turning to smash home winners, flashed through her mind. It had been her legs that had been her greatest physical strength. No one could match her lower-body power. Roxy felt pride fill her chest. She wasn't a textbook case. She was Roxy Campbell. A champion. And she would show them the power that she had inside her.

She manoeuvred her body to the side of the bed so that her legs were hanging over the edge. She took five deep breaths and visualized all her strength centring in her legs. She imagined them being stronger than they had ever been. She imagined them being sturdy enough to support the weight of a house. Then she pushed herself off the bed and waited for her legs to spring back to life.

There was an almighty crash as she fell, smacking her arms and the back of her head against the frame of the bed. She had not been able to cushion her fall in any way. When the door opened and Malin dashed in, Roxy was lying in a heap on the floor, crying.

SATURDAY
21st JULY

'Kaine?' said Mr Kerrigan, opening his front door and checking his watch. 'It's quite late. Shouldn't you be at home?'

'It's Roxy,' said Kaine, grabbing at his teacher's arm. 'She can't walk . . . She's never going to be able to walk again . . .'

'No!' gasped Mr Kerrigan, reaching forward to put a hand on Kaine's shoulder.

'I'm sorry for coming here, but . . . I didn't know where to go.'

'It's OK. Of course it's OK. Come in.' Mr Kerrigan led him in and sat him down on the sofa. 'Here,' he said, handing Kaine a glass. 'Drink some water.'

'They did another operation . . .' Kaine said through his tears, 'and they found out her back was damaged. It's permanent, sir . . .'

Mr Kerrigan shook his head and for a few moments they sat in silence.

'How . . . unbelievably sad,' said Mr Kerrigan. 'And her tennis too . . . She was so gifted. I genuinely thought Roxy would win Wimbledon one day. I'm so, so sorry, Kaine. It's a ridiculous question, I know, but . . . how is she? How's she coping?'

Kaine shook his head. 'She's not. None of us are. I can't stop thinking about her, sir. My brain . . . is . . . and the trial . . . How am I supposed to play now? Will you tell them, sir? Will you tell Southampton why I can't play?'

Mr Kerrigan looked at Kaine with a gentle expression. 'If you want me to do that, I will,' he said. 'It's your decision, and I can't imagine what you're feeling right now, but . . . I just wonder whether there might be another way to think about this. Maybe, what you need, what your family needs, what *Roxy* needs right now is some good news. Something positive to concentrate on. Maybe that's what this trial is. Your chance to bring some light.'

Kaine took in a deep breath and looked around him.

As he dried his eyes with his T-shirt, he noticed how untidy Mr K's flat was. Though it was a strange thought to have at that time, he realized that he had always assumed that teachers would live in really neat homes, but Mr K's place was just as messy as Kaine's bedroom.

'I think you should play in the trial, Kaine,' said Mr K. 'For what it's worth, that's my view. More than anything, this shows that you've got to grab an opportunity when it comes along. There might not be a second chance.'

Kaine closed his eyes. He could feel his pulse starting to slow down a little. 'If I did, sir . . . If I did play, would you come?' he asked. 'When you're there . . . I feel safe.'

'When is it?' asked Mr Kerrigan.

'Sunday, sir. Next week. The twenty-ninth. Two o'clock.'

'Erm, let me check my diary . . .' said Mr K, picking up his Compton Academy diary. 'Taking the wife and kids on holiday . . . ? No. They don't exist. Taking the girlfriend for a romantic stroll in the country . . . ? Nope. She doesn't exist either. Turns out I'm free. Yes, if you play, Kaine . . . one hundred per cent I'll be there.'

'Thanks, sir,' said Kaine. 'I'll think about it. I need to try and get my head around everything.'

'Do it for Roxy,' said Mr K. 'Give her something to cheer.'

They walked to the door and Mr K gave Kaine's shoulder a squeeze of encouragement. 'Do you want me to walk you home?' he asked. 'It'll be getting dark soon.'

'It's all right, sir,' said Kaine. 'Don't worry. I'll be OK. I'll go straight home.'

'Good man, Kaine,' he said. 'You're going to be OK. And, somehow, I believe Roxy's going to be OK too.'

Kaine looked at his teacher. 'By the way, Mr K,' he said '. . . if you do become a dad, you're going to be a brilliant one.'

On his way home, Kaine felt his mind starting to get a bit clearer. Mr K knew how to make him feel calm. He got out his phone to text his dad to say he'd be back soon and to ask if they could then drive over and see Roxy. He was just about to start texting when a message came through from a withheld number.

> You think you can just turn your back and walk away?
> You know better than that.
> SS

Sunday July 22
<u>4 days since I woke up . . .</u>

Diary,
Kaine has just given you back to me.

I guess you know what happened. Turns out I've got something called vascular myelopathy in my back. I'll hate those two words for ever because they have ended my life.

I'm a lump of flesh sat on a chair. That's who I am, all day every day. I try to pretend I'm all right when Mum and Dad and Kaine come. I tell them I'm getting used to things and that it'll be OK. That way it keeps the conversations shorter. But as soon as they leave my brain starts poisoning me from the inside and my heart burns with anger that feels like it's come straight from hell.

All I do, every day, is wait to go to sleep so that it'll all be over for a few hours. I wish it was over for ever. As soon as I wake up, I know. The sickness hits me first and then my mind catches up.

255

I'm never going to be able to walk again. And I'm never going to be able to play t— I can't even write it. I can't even think about it. I feel like I'm going to wake up one day and this will all be finished. It will all have been a dream. Because if it's real . . . I just can't . . .

Nothing matters any more. I don't care about anything. I don't even care about trying to stop AJ from visiting me.

It's good. He can see how ugly I look with my scars all over my head. He can see how helpless I am sitting in my wheelchair. The more he sees the truth, the quicker he'll just leave me alone.

We just sit there in silence. That's the way I like it.

It's the only time someone's not lying.

WEDNESDAY
25th JULY

It was early in the morning and Roxy looked at the text she had just received.

It was not one she had been expecting.

> Hi Roxy,
> It's Annabelle Taylor.
> No problem if you don't want to, but I'm in reception downstairs and I would really like to see you if that would be ok.
> Sorry to disturb you.
> Annabelle

She texted back:

> Hi.
> Am on the 8th floor.
> They'll show you which is my room.
> R

'Knock, knock,' said Annabelle as she poked her head around the door to Roxy's room a few minutes later.

'Hi,' said Roxy, wheeling herself around. She immediately saw the shock on Annabelle's face when she caught sight of the scars on Roxy's head.

'I brought you these,' said Annabelle. She placed a huge bouquet of flowers in a jug by Roxy's bed.

'Thanks,' said Roxy.

Annabelle sat down, and for a long time there was silence.

'I had to come and see you,' she said finally. 'I think about you every day. I'm so . . . sorry.'

'Thanks,' said Roxy.

'And also, I wanted to apologize,' said Annabelle. 'For the things I said to you. It was wrong.'

'It's fine,' said Roxy. 'Doesn't matter any more anyway.'

She couldn't bear to look Annabelle in the face. Just seeing her brought back all the tennis memories.

'I keep thinking . . .' said Annabelle, 'if we hadn't played, if we hadn't pushed each other so hard, then it would never have happen—'

'It had nothing to do with that,' said Roxy. 'It was inside me for a long time. We just didn't know.'

Once again, there was silence.

'I don't know whether it's the right thing to say now or not . . .' said Annabelle, 'but the way you played in that game . . . the way you fought . . . You were a beast. The best I've ever played against.'

Roxy nodded and wheeled herself over to the window. She looked outside at the cars driving down the road. 'The last few months,' she said, 'I didn't even think I liked tennis . . .'

She turned and looked at Annabelle, who was nodding. She understood.

'I thought that I didn't want it,' Roxy said. 'But in that game, I made it *my* dream again. And when I did, it was like I woke up . . . But the minute I realized how much I wanted it . . . ' She tried to smile but she couldn't. 'Thanks for coming, Annabelle. And good luck with your tennis,' she said. 'I'd like to be by myself now.'

Kaine waited until Roxy's visitor had left the room. Then he went in.

'Hey,' he said. Roxy was sitting in her chair staring out of the window, but she didn't turn around or acknowledge him coming in.

'Roxy,' he said cautiously. 'I've been thinking about the trial . . . you know, at Southampton. And . . . I was wondering whether you wanted to come and . . . watch?'

She still didn't turn round. In his mind, he tried to get inside her head, to feel what she was thinking, but there was nothing coming back. She was a brick wall. He saw her shift in her wheelchair.

'I don't think I'm allowed to leave the hospital yet,' she said.

'No, it's cool,' said Kaine. 'I already asked the doctor. He said it's fine if one of the nurses comes . . . I bet you must be dying to get outside?'

Roxy shook her head.

'You know, it would be the biggest inspiration I could ever have,' Kaine said. 'To have you there . . . to give you something to . . . cheer.'

Roxy didn't answer so Kaine walked over to stand next to her. He could see she was crying.

'It's not the right time, Kaine,' she said, wheeling herself away from him. 'I've got a lot of stuff to deal with right now. You don't need me there. You'll be fine.'

She wheeled herself into the bathroom and shut the door.

Kaine closed his eyes and felt his stomach sink. 'OK,' he called out to her, trying not to sound too disappointed.

He tried to think back to all the promises he had made himself when Roxy had been unconscious; they would go back to being as close as they had been when they were younger, neither of them would ever feel alone again . . . But now, even though she was only in the next room, Roxy felt a million miles away.

Samantha was unloading the shopping into the fridge. As she did so, she noticed that Kaine had put the old family photo back into its frame on the windowsill. It was her favourite photo because every single member of the family looked genuinely happy. It was such a long time ago. She wondered whether they might ever be able to take another photo in which the whole family looked happy.

Three slow, hard knocks at the door gave her a jolt. Opening it, she found a man standing outside, smoking a cigar; he was wearing a smart suit and she immediately knew who he was. Without saying a word, she left the door open and watched Sheldon Statham walk into her flat. She felt the hairs on the back of her neck stand up.

'Sorry to hear about your daughter,' he said, looking around. 'Great shame.'

Looking at him, Samantha was struck by how small he was, face to face. She had expected him to be bigger in person.

'I want you to stay away from my family,' she said. 'I'll give you the two hundred pounds Kaine owes you – and more – and then I want you to leave us alone.'

Sheldon Statham laughed, blowing the smoke from his cigar directly into her face.

'You've picked on the wrong family and the wrong mother at the wrong time,' she said. 'Who do you think you are?'

'Who am I?' said Sheldon, speaking extremely slowly. He took another deep drag on his cigar. 'I think you know who I am.'

'You think I'm scared of *you*?' Samantha said. 'I've lived with death since I was eight years old. It doesn't scare me. But my children – as long as I'm alive I will never let you anywhere near them. What will it take for you to leave us alone?'

Sheldon did not answer. He just stared at Samantha, smiling at her.

'Wait there,' she said.

She went into her bedroom, got out the black box and took out all the money she had left after selling her mother's wedding ring, and paying the bills.

'Here,' she said, coming back in, holding all the notes in her hands.

He was busy looking at the photos of her as a child. He seemed to be distracted.

'Here!' she said again, thrusting the money at him. 'It's over five hundred pounds – that's it – every last penny we have. I hope it makes you happy.'

Sheldon took the money and folded it into one neat stack.

'You'll leave him alone now? This is finished?'

'Finished . . . ?' said Sheldon. 'Why would it be finished?'

'Because I told you, that's all we've got,' said Samantha. 'There's nothing else.' She looked Sheldon Statham dead in the eye. 'You think you're somebody,' she said. 'But you're not. You are a nothing. You need to be surrounded by your gang, your boys, to feel like you've got power. But, by yourself, as an individual, you are one of the most pitiful human beings I have ever come across. And deep down you know it.'

She stood face to face with him and glared at him. She didn't give one inch even when, once again, he blew smoke directly in her eyes.

After a few seconds, Sheldon leaned down and put his cigar out on the tablecloth. 'It's been a long time since I've seen you, Samantha,' he said. 'I won't leave it so long next time.'

She watched him leave the flat, and as soon as he did, she rushed to the door, slammed it shut and double-locked it, before slumping down to the floor. She was breathing so fast she felt as though she might pass out.

Above having him in her flat, above giving him over a five hundred pounds, there was one thing that he had said that had made her feel truly sick, and she couldn't get it out of her mind. *It's been a long time since I've seen you* . . . What did he mean? She had never met him before in her—

Suddenly her blood ran cold and her heart stopped beating. She had a dead feeling, deep inside her chest. Her memory flashed back to the darkest day of her life. She saw in her mind's eye what she had seen that day. *Who* she had seen that day. With shaking hands, she raised herself back up from the floor and went into her bedroom. She put the black box on her bed and took out every single one of her mother's files.

Roxy checked the time on her phone. 5.04 p.m. She lifted her phone above her and, without bothering to smile, she took a selfie. She wanted to know what she truly looked like. Seeing Annabelle that morning had reminded her of what she used to be: a winner capable of slugging it out with the best players in the country. But who was she now?

Staring at the photo she had just taken, all she could see was a small, weak-looking girl with an ugly scar all the way down the side of her skull. The girl's body looked lost in the big wheelchair and her frame seemed so thin and fragile that anyone might snap her spine if they just hugged her.

Roxy wheeled herself back towards her bed. If she could get to sleep, the agony would go away for a little while. But before she could get there, she stopped in the middle of the room and began to cry. At first it was quiet and then it turned into huge, violent roars of pain.

'Why?' she shouted, punching the arms of her wheelchair over and over again. 'Why? Why? *Why?*'

'Oh, Roxy,' said Malin, coming in. She hugged Roxy while she cried. 'Talk to me,' she said. 'Tell me how you're feeling.'

'It's over,' said Roxy through her tears. 'My life is

over and . . . I can't bear the fact that everyone else is just getting on with theirs. Annabelle's got her tennis. Kaine's going to be a professional footballer . . . and I'm going to be stuck in a chair for the rest of my life. I hate everyone, including myself. I won't even go and support Kaine on Sunday. I can't. I can't bear to watch it.' She punched her own legs to see if she could feel any pain, but there was nothing.

'You need to go through this,' said Malin, gently taking hold of Roxy's hand. 'You need to feel it.'

'What do you mean I *need to feel it*?' shouted Roxy. 'What do I need to feel? What's the point in feeling anything? My life is over!'

'You think it is,' said Malin. 'But trust me, it's not. Everyone says you're a fighter. Well, this is a fight all right, Roxy. The biggest fight of your life.'

'What do you know about *my* life, Malin? Tell me! Do you know I sacrificed my whole life – all my friends, everything – for tennis? And now tennis is gone. So what have I got left? Nothing. I've been cheated out of my whole life! You want me to fight? How am I supposed to fight when I can't even walk?'

Malin nodded to Roxy to encourage her to keep talking. 'Carry on,' she said. 'I'm listening.'

Roxy looked at Malin. 'Number one in the world,' she said. She was still crying, but more softly now. 'Winning Wimbledon. I truly believe I could have done both of them. Done everything. Been the best. I was just getting started. I'm not ready for it to end. I just can't believe it's all . . . over.'

'I'm going to be straight with you,' said Malin. 'The way you thought your life was going to be, it's gone. You're right. That life, the way you wanted it, it's not available. It's hard to say it, but it's true. But that *doesn't* mean it's *all* over.' Malin squeezed Roxy's hand tight. 'Roxy,' she said. 'You can still be everything you want to be.'

Roxy looked at Malin and tried to understand.

'But how?' she said. 'I don't know how.'

'Hey, Mum,' said Kaine as he heard Samantha coming in that evening. 'Where have you been? I tried to call you, but it went straight to voicemail.'

He watched her as she put her jacket on the chair by the kitchen table. He had never seen her look so tired. She looked completely washed out.

'Are you OK?' he asked.

'Yes,' she said. 'Just been a very . . . full-on day.' She was looking at her hands, which had ink stains on them. She walked to the sink to wash them.

'Did you see I put the photo back?' said Kaine.

'I did,' she said softly. 'Thank you.'

Kaine could see his mum was so drained that she almost could not speak. He went up and hugged her. As he did so, he noticed that she smelled different but somehow familiar. It took him a while to realize what it was. And then it struck him; her clothes smelled of cigar smoke.

He took a step back and stared at her. She nodded back as if to confirm his thoughts. Kaine understood what had happened. She had gone into the spider's web for him.

THURSDAY
26th JULY

Kaine looked out of his bedroom window and up at the stars. He tried to find the brightest, most beautiful one. 'Hi, Mamma,' he said.

With two days to go until the trial, he had started to think about her more and more. She was the one who had predicted he would become a footballer, and she was the one who had always believed in him. He wished she was here now to calm him down and help him with all the different emotions he was feeling. The nerves about the trial itself . . . the guilt about the possibility of achieving his dreams when Roxy was living a nightmare. At times, it had become too much for him to deal with.

He had stopped eating proper meals and his thoughts had become a tangled mess. To try to soothe his internal doubts and fears, he decided to remind himself of the last time he spoke to Mamma. It was at her funeral, when he gave a short speech. He had spoken it as if he was talking directly to her, which was exactly what he needed to do now. He went to his desk and took out the speech, which he had written himself and practised saying out loud in the week leading up to the funeral.

Thank you Mamma
Thank you ~~for~~ for the love you gave me and for making me believe that something more than the ordinary is possible
I know it is, ~~beca~~ because you were never ordinary
I ll miss you so much but I know where ~~you~~ you are
You always used to talk about the stars on your island and how beautiful they are
I know that you are one of ~~those~~ those stars now

I ll always look for you and in my life I ll try to stand up as tall as I can to reach you
I ll see you ~~~~ again one day Mamma and until then
I ll try to make you proud by becoming the person you said I would be

Kaine

FRIDAY
27ᵗʰ JULY

'Hey,' said Daryll, poking his head around the door. 'Thought I'd check in. How you feeling?'

'I'm OK,' said Roxy, wheeling herself towards her dad. 'Malin says I can probably come home in a few days.'

'I heard,' said Daryll. 'That's what we all want. To get you home as soon as possible.'

Roxy tried to imagine herself going back to her room. The room that she had left that Sunday morning with no idea that she would never be able to walk back into it.

'Kaine ready for the trial?' she asked.

'I think so . . .' said Daryll. There was silence. 'At least he doesn't have to worry about me raving on at him from the sidelines any more,' he said. 'I've . . . stopped doing that, Roxy.'

Roxy hung her head. 'What I would give to have you shouting at me while I trained now,' she said.

Quietly, they sat together, both trying to hold back their tears.

'I'm not going to the trial,' she said.

'I know,' said Daryll. 'Kaine told me. It's OK. You don't have to do anything you don't want to. Watching other people play sport right now is probably . . .' He stopped talking and took a deep breath. 'Roxy,' he said. 'I just want you to know . . . how sorry I am for . . . the way I was with you over the last few months . . . the way I pushed you. I just . . .' He paused and covered his eyes with his thumb and his forefinger. 'I didn't have a job. I couldn't provide for the family. I felt . . . inadequate . . . and I took it out on you. I know I did.'

Roxy watched as Daryll started crying. She held his hand.

'It's OK, Dad,' she said. 'It's OK . . .'

'Your tennis,' he said. 'You were . . . so good . . . so brilliant. I thought it could be the answer. For all of us. But I pushed it too far. I pushed *you* too far.'

She recognized the expression on his face. She had

been there herself. She could see in his eyes that, at that moment, he hated tennis.

'Hey,' she said. He was shaking his head. He couldn't hear her. 'Hey!' she said again. 'Don't blame yourself, Dad. It happened – but it wasn't because of you . . . OK? And don't blame tennis either. I love that sport. It was my dream. Do you hear me? *My* dream . . .'

She hugged her dad, and as she felt the depth of his sadness, she sensed the words that Malin had said rising up within her again. Those words – *You can still be everything you want to be* – had been reverberating around her head constantly for the last forty-eight hours.

'Dad . . .' she said hesitantly. 'I think . . . it still *is* my dream.'

'Wow!' said Queenie as Kaine walked out of the barber's. 'You look great!'

'Hey, Queenie,' said Kaine. They hadn't arranged to meet up, but Kaine had long since stopped being surprised by his friend's ability to pop up out of nowhere. 'I'm heading home,' he added. 'Wanna walk with me?'

Queenie nodded enthusiastically, and they headed back in the general direction of the estate, with Kaine setting a rapid pace. Earlier in the evening, he'd popped into AJ's to invite him to come in the car with them and watch the game on Sunday. Then he'd gone to the barber's to get a new cut for the trial, but because there'd been a queue, it had taken longer than he'd expected. It was now already dark.

'You're going to do so well in the trial,' said Queenie as they entered the park. 'I just know it. Are you feeling excited?'

But Kaine wasn't listening. Further down the path, he could see five boys, all wearing hoodies, running directly towards them. In the light of the street lamp, he could see something glinting in one of the boy's hands. It was the blade of a knife. For a second he stopped breathing. He was rooted to the spot. The gang was getting closer.

They were shouting as they ran. Without thinking, he pushed Queenie into the railings and huddled down next to him so that they could not be seen.

'What's goin—'

Kaine put his hand over Queenie's mouth and put his finger over his lips for him to be quiet. Then, sprinting along the path in front of them came the group of five boys. Under their hoodies, they all had their faces covered with bandanas, and as they ran past, Kaine could see that he had been right; one of them was holding a big sharp knife.

'What's going on?' said Queenie, once they'd gone. 'Who were they?'

'Not sure,' said Kaine. 'Compton Estate gang, I reckon. Sheldon's boys. I thought . . . they might be coming for me – but I think they were after someone else.'

Kaine hauled Queenie back to his feet and looked all around to make sure that the other boys had definitely gone.

'Kaine,' said Queenie. His face was as white as a sheet. 'I'm scared.'

Kaine nodded. He could feel his heart thumping like a drum in his chest. 'Let's get home quickly,' he said.

They raced through the park, running in the opposite direction from where Sheldon's gang had gone. They were just about to reach the exit when they saw a body, slumped on the ground under a tree.

It was almost pitch-black now, but Kaine could still see the thick dark liquid that was seeping out from underneath the body, staining the dry earth. Blood.

The two boys looked at each other.

'Come on,' said Kaine, pulling at Queenie's coat. 'We can't leave them like this. Hello?' he said to the figure, who was lying face down in the ground. 'Can you hear me? You need to get to the hospital.'

The body did not move. Kaine rolled it over. It was a boy, wearing a hoodie. His clothes were soaked in warm, sticky blood. It was everywhere.

'Kaine,' said Queenie. 'I don't want to be here. They might come back. We need to go. Now!'

'He's still breathing!' said Kaine. 'We can't leave him.' He pulled back the boy's hood and instantly recognized the face he saw: Rufus Blackstock.

Suddenly Rufus's eyes opened and he grabbed Kaine's arm. 'Help,' he whispered, staring straight at Kaine.

'What happened?' asked Kaine. 'Did Sheldon send them?'

Rufus tried to answer, but he couldn't speak. His lips were almost blue and there was blood coming out of his mouth. He nodded and pointed to his belly. When Kaine lifted the top, he could see two deep stab wounds, right in the middle of Rufus's stomach. Blood was still gushing out.

'What do we do?' said Queenie, looking on in horror. 'He looks like he's going to . . .'

The sight of Rufus lying stricken on the ground triggered a million images and memories. They flooded Kaine's mind all at once: arguing with Rufus on the football court . . . Sheldon . . . Roxy . . . Uncle Anthony . . . Mamma . . . the way he'd panicked when he had found her . . . lying there.

'Stay calm, Queenie,' he said firmly. He took off his jacket and chucked Queenie his phone. 'You call 999,' he said. 'I'm going to put pressure on it so no more blood gets out.' He covered the wound with his jacket and pushed down as hard as he could. 'Stay with me, Rufus!' he said. 'Keep your eyes open and stay with me. It's going to be OK . . .'

SUNDAY
29th JULY

R oxy took a deep breath.

Then, with her heart beating faster than when she'd been serving for the County Finals, she pressed 'send'. She covered her eyes and let out a high-pitched yelp of excitement as she imagined her text travelling through the air and being delivered direct to AJ's phone. She had spent the last half an hour writing him a note, taking a photo of what she'd written and texting it over to him:

Alonso,

Happy Sunday!

Right, it's time to get real with you, boy. I'm fed up of wasting time.

I like you. You know I do.

When I get out of hospital do you want to go and see a film with me? Just us.

Please circle your answer:

- Yes I want to go to the cinema with you

- Yes I REALLY want to go to the cinema with you

PS - You can tell Kaine or whoever you want about this. I don't care!

PPS - I don't share popcorn so don't try any funny stuff

Rx

'Are you OK, Roxy?' called Malin, rushing into the room. 'I thought I heard a scream. Is everything all right?'

'Yeah, I am OK actually,' said Roxy. She could feel herself blushing. 'I just did something . . . well, like you said, it's time to start being who I want to be.'

'Good,' said Malin. 'And I'm glad to see you're

already up and dressed because we should probably get going.'

'What are you talking about?' Roxy said.

'Well . . . I think it'll do you good to get out of this stuffy room, don't you?'

'To go where?' said Roxy. 'If we're going outside I need to get ready.'

'Don't worry,' said Malin. 'You're plenty ready.'

It was eleven o'clock on the morning of the trial and Kaine was pacing his room, trying to stay calm. His dad had said he was going to pick up Mr K and then they would come back to collect Kaine, Samantha and AJ for the drive down to Southampton. But he had left fifteen minutes ago and Mr K only lived five minutes away . . .

His frenzied thoughts were interrupted when his phone started ringing. He didn't know the number so he let it ring out. Thirty seconds later it pinged to tell him he had a message. He really didn't want to listen to it in case it was Sheldon or one of the Compton gang, but he was scared that something might have happened to his dad . . . He called his voicemail and, with his hand trembling, lifted the phone to his ear.

Kaine . . . it's Rufus here. I just wanted to say . . . thanks. They said I lost so much blood that if it'd been another ten minutes . . . I would've died. But they say I'm gonna be OK. Thanks to you. And your friend. Look . . . I know a lot of stuff has gone on with you and me but . . . that's finished now, all right? . . . I've got quite a lot of thinking to do . . . I'll see you round, OK, Kaine?

Kaine closed his eyes and let out a long, deep breath.

He could feel one of his biggest fears slowly starting to dissolve. He texted Rufus back:

> Thanks for your message Rufus.
> Get well and yeah see you round.
> Kaine

Then he texted Queenie:

> Rufus gonna be ok.
> Thanks to you.
> You were cool when it mattered.
> K

He had just sent the text when, finally, he heard a hoot coming from outside. He quickly grabbed his new boots and followed his mum down the steps towards the car park. He was surprised to see the school mini-bus there, chugging away. When he looked closer, he could see that his dad and Mr K were in the front, waving.

Kaine sprinted over to the window. 'Dad,' he said. 'What are you doing in this?'

His dad smiled and pointed his thumb backwards. There in the back of the van were Roxy, Malin and AJ.

'I can't believe it!' Kaine said, running round to the back. 'You're all here! My man,' he beamed, fist-bumping with AJ as he leaped into the van. 'Roxy!' he said. 'But what are you doing here? I thought you weren't going to come.'

'Well, Malin made me realize I'd made a terrible mistake,' she said. 'There's no way you're good enough to play in this match without my power too. So I'm here to give it to you.'

Kaine gave his sister the biggest hug and sat down next to her. Although she seemed a lot better than she had been, he could tell that she still wished so badly that she was out there playing today too.

'I really appreciate you being here, Sis,' he said softly. 'It makes it . . . complete.'

After half an hour of the journey, everyone had stopped talking to allow Kaine some time to get his mind on the game, but the silence only made him more nervous.

'So,' he said, to no one and everyone. 'Anyone going to tell me how you all arranged this? I bet no one else will be turning up with a whole minibus of support today.'

'Guilty,' said Malin, smiling. 'Your dad gave me the number for the Mr Kerrigan that your family spend so much time talking about, and between the two of us, we made a little plan, didn't we, Noel?'

Mr K nodded from the front.

'But I must say,' she continued, pretending to whisper but speaking just as loudly as before, 'I'm quite angry with you Campbells. How come none of you thought to tell me that he was such a dish? I haven't even got my make-up on, have I?' She took out her little hand mirror and started busily fussing with the fringe of her thick red hair.

Kaine looked to the front to see that Mr K's face had gone a deep beetroot colour. He squeezed his teacher's shoulder and started laughing. As he did so, he could feel his nerves disappearing into the distance.

Twenty minutes later, the lush green country roads led them to a sign which said *Southampton FC, Staplewood Campus* and a man on the gate lifted the barrier to let them in. As soon as they parked, Kaine jumped out and started loosening up his muscles. He watched as Malin placed the ramp down between the minibus and the ground for Roxy to wheel herself down.

'Is it OK if I do that?' AJ asked Malin, who smiled and stepped to the side.

As he saw AJ carefully place the ramp down and then gently help Roxy out, Kaine noticed the way his sister was looking up at AJ. Instantly, he could detect something. They were talking and laughing together – and it was her real laugh. Her happy laugh. He didn't know what had occurred but he was certain that something had passed between the two of them. He thought back to how angry he used to be whenever AJ asked him about Roxy but now, as he saw that energy between them, he felt like hugging his best friend and congratulating him on being with the best girl in the world.

Staplewood Training Ground
Southampton Football Club
Trial Match

With ten minutes until kickoff, Kaine did his warm-up and looked around him. The training ground was probably the most beautiful place he had ever seen in his life. Row upon row of immaculate pitches, all freshly mown and painted. He inhaled the smell of the cut grass and thought about the gravelly court he and AJ kicked about on every night at the estate. *If I can't play here, I can't play anywhere.*

He took his position in the middle of the pitch and scanned both teams to see who was on his side and who he was up against. The two teams were made up of a mixture of the existing Southampton Under-14 squad plus four or five players who had, like Kaine, been invited down for a trial. He had already acknowledged a couple of the boys whose faces he knew from school matches or weekend games with his club. Everyone had been pretty friendly, apart from one boy with pale skin and really spiky black hair. He seemed to be trying to stare Kaine down all the time for no reason . . .

Kaine didn't know who the boy was or what his

problem was, but if he was trying to put him off he had no chance. Kaine had come to play today and that was what he was going to do.

The match started terribly. Kaine could feel the jitters within himself right from the kickoff. He was sweating all over his body, and when the ball came to him for the first time, he was so nervous about making a mistake that he held onto it for too long and lost possession.

He cursed himself and worried that his dad would start shouting at him in front of everyone, but when he looked over Daryll was just smiling. He didn't say a word. Instead, he just gave Kaine the thumbs up.

Kaine felt his composure coming back. As soon as he put his foot on the gas and sprinted after a ball, he could hear some of the people in the crowd gasp at his speed. Then, after he played a long diagonal pass, which landed inch-perfectly at the feet of the overlapping right back, he saw Brian, the scout, and the Academy Director pointing at him, talking and nodding their heads.

Everything good. Nearly.

The only problem was the boy with the spiky hair. He was fouling Kaine all the time. Snide little ones;

leaving his foot in after the ball had gone, shirt pulling, tripping Kaine as he was breaking forward. By themselves, they weren't anything serious, but put together, they were starting to annoy Kaine.

It looked like Mr Kerrigan had spotted what was happening too.

'Stay cool, my man,' he said, jogging to catch up with Kaine as the referee blew his whistle for half time. 'You're bossing this. Best player on the park. Ignore that kid. This is too important for you. Do you get me?'

'I get you,' said Kaine.

But sure enough, within only a couple of minutes of the restart, the next foul came when the boy blatantly tripped Kaine up.

'Sorry, mate,' he said, helping Kaine to his feet, but when Kaine started to jog away, the boy flicked Kaine really hard in the ear. Kaine immediately turned round and stared hard at the boy. Every part of him wanted to react, but he kept himself under control. Just.

'Cut it out, you two,' said the referee, coming in between them. Then, as soon as play carried on, the boy trod on the back of Kaine's heel, making one of his new boots come off.

'Are you going to do something about this, referee?'

Mr Kerrigan suddenly yelled from the touchline. 'Am I the only one who's clocked what's happening here?! If you don't deal with it, then I will!'

Kaine could see that his teacher's head had gone. His clear blue eyes were now red with rage. He looked as though he was about to enter the field of play to tell the boy what he thought of him. But before he could, a very strong set of arms stopped him.

'It's OK, Noel,' said Daryll, calmly but firmly easing Mr Kerrigan away from the touchline. 'Kaine's got this.'

The longer the match went on, the more comfortable Kaine felt. He kept his midfield game simple and efficient; passing sensibly, retaining possession and protecting the defence. And when the opportunity arose, he set up opportunities for the attackers too. All without reacting to the provocation from the boy with the spiky hair. Kaine had done everything right. But nothing special.

Then, with two minutes left in the game, he intercepted a loose ball and strode forwards, beating a man by jinking past him on the halfway line. He advanced a further couple of paces before he became aware that the boy with spiky hair was sprinting towards him and was about to make a tackle.

Kaine had a millisecond to decide what he was going to do. He was forty yards out from goal and there was an easy, simple pass available to him to his left. Did he want to go for broke or keep the ball? How did he want to end this trial match? If he took on a shot now – from all this way out – and missed, he would look selfish, arrogant and wasteful. But if he scored, from here, it would be a moment that no one would forget. Or should he go for the middle option and try a slightly more adventurous pass than the simple dink out wide?

Safe or risky? Simple or special? As the boy's aggressive tackle came flying in, there was no more time to decide. Kaine knew that this was it. He could feel his family and supporters on the sideline lean forward. And he was certain he could sense Mamma looking down on him too . . .

This moment would decide his football future, and deep down, he knew that he was never going to do it the ordinary way.

He told himself: *Smash it! Smash it with everything you've got.* Then he hammered his foot through the ball and watched as it exploded off his boot. *Please*, he said aloud, as he tracked its flight. *Get in that goal.*

The ball scorched through the air like a laser. It seemed to get faster and faster as it flew forwards. Everyone on the pitch and those watching on the touchline stopped moving and focused on the missile heading for the goal. The keeper made a step to his right, but he was too late. He could only look up as the ball soared into the roof of the net, almost breaking the frame of the goal in the process.

'Yes!!' Kaine shouted, leaping into the air. Pure joy was sizzling throughout his body.

'*That's* what I'm talking about!' Roxy roared,

punching her fist into the air. 'Proper Campbell power! You don't stop that!'

Kaine turned to his sister, clenched his own fist, and nodded to her. He was sure that his shot had had both their power behind it.

Kaine's strike was the only goal of the game, and when the final whistle went, he was leaning forwards, panting, trying to get his breath back. Whatever the club now decided was out of his hands. He knew he had given everything he had to give. There was just one final thing he still needed to do.

'Hey! Yo!' he called out, running after the boy with spiky black hair as the players walked off the pitch. The boy turned round and looked up at Kaine. Kaine could see that he was scared.

'Well played,' Kaine said to the boy. 'No hard feelings.'

The boy looked relieved. 'Well played to you,' he said.

'There you are,' said Brian, coming up to the two boys. 'Ah, Kaine, I see you've already met Jackson . . . That's probably just as well because I have a little admission to make . . . Jackson is one of our boys and I asked him to put himself about a bit as far as you were concerned today. Nothing too serious, but I just wanted him to make life uncomfortable for you, to see how your temperament was under a bit of pressure . . . A bit cheeky of us, I know, but it was the only way we could tell if you'd come on as much as I thought you had. Jackson's a good lad really.'

'Ah . . . right,' said Kaine, feeling a lot of his questions about the boy disappear. 'OK.'

'Sorry,' said Jackson, with an embarrassed smile. 'Well done for not taking the bait, though. You must have thought I was a proper wind-up merchant. Great goal by, the way.'

'Kaine,' said Brian, putting his arm round Kaine's shoulder. 'There's someone else I'd like you to meet. This is Ivan Baldwin, our Academy Director.'

Kaine turned around and shielded his eyes from the sun. He saw a man purposefully stride towards him.

'Pleasure to meet you,' said Ivan Baldwin, stretching out his hand.

'Nice to meet you too,' said Kaine, shaking his hand firmly, keeping positive eye contact throughout. 'Thanks for inviting me to play.'

'Kaine, I think you can probably guess what I'm going

to say. You played extremely well today. Excellently, in fact. And that was . . . some goal. I would very much like to sign you up to play for our Under-Fifteens squad next season. What do you say?'

'I say yes!' said Kaine, beaming from ear to ear. He could feel his body glowing with pride. 'It would be an honour.'

'Good,' said Mr Baldwin. 'I'm excited to get you on board. We'll get everything organized with your parents. It was great to see them here supporting you today.'

'Brilliant,' said Kaine. He had never felt a well of such deep happiness. 'I guess I'll see you next season then, Mr Baldwin.'

'Oh, before you go, I've just got one question for you,' said the Academy Director. 'We've got scouts travelling all over the place, every single day watching games . . . we've got a database of every player out there, so how on earth is it that we haven't had you down here to play before now?'

Kaine looked at the man and smiled. 'I wasn't ready, Mr Baldwin,' he said. 'But I am now.'

While the Academy Director introduced himself to Daryll and Samantha, Kaine ran towards Mr Kerrigan.

'I did it!' he shouted, leaping all over his teacher. 'They're going to sign me, sir! And it's all because of you!'

'I knew it!' Mr Kerrigan said. 'Well done! You were incredible today, Kaine! And that goal – where did that come from?'

Kaine looked up at the sky and smiled. 'But, sir,' he said, suddenly looking doubtful again. 'What happens next? Can I come over to yours next week to make a plan for when I join up properly? I'll be playing for the Under-Fifteens . . . can we talk tactics?'

Mr Kerrigan smiled, but it looked like a happy-sad smile. 'Kaine,' he said. 'I'm going to say something now which . . . Look, you know I'm always here for you. That's for keeps. But I have a feeling that the best person you can have these kind of chats with now is your dad . . .'

Kaine looked down at the ground. His throat hurt.

'Don't worry, I'm not going anywhere,' said Mr Kerrigan. 'But . . . Daryll's your dad, Kaine. Let him be that.'

Mr K put his hand on Kaine's shoulder and pointed behind him. As Kaine turned around, he saw that his family was now coming towards him.

'I'm so proud of you, Kaine,' his dad said. 'I'm so proud of both of you.'

Daryll gave Kaine and Roxy a huge bear hug, then widened his arms further to pull Samantha in too. From underneath the tree of their dad's big, solid arms, Roxy and Kaine gave each other a high-five. Their timing was perfect.

'Everybody look this way!' Mr Kerrigan said.

The Campbells all looked up to see Mr Kerrigan pointing his phone in their direction. He took a photo. A new family photo.

THE END

EPILOGUE

ONE WEEK LATER

ANTHONY AUGUSTINE SUSPECT ARRESTED

A man has been charged with the murder of Anthony Augustine, the 14-year-old boy whose life was taken close to the Compton Estate, thirty years ago.

Sheldon Statham, 46, has been charged with murder after his DNA samples matched those found at the scene three decades ago. The arrest and charge comes following a new statement made by the only witness to the crime, Samantha Campbell, Augustine's sister.

Augustine, a talented and much-liked student, was tragically stabbed to death in a case of mistaken identity, by a gang fighting for control of the Compton Estate area.

"We hope that justice – a justice my mother searched so long for – will now be done," said Campbell. "My brother was an angel. We dearly miss him every day and, while nothing will bring him back, we hope that both he and my mother can now rest in peace."

Statham will face trial for the murder, news which has been welcomed by local police, who believe he heads up one of the most dangerous gangs in the area, employing children as young as eleven and twelve to carry out serious crime.

"This arrest was only possible thanks to the bravery of Samantha Campbell," said Detective Superintendent, Marcus Forde. "There is a culture

Cri for

"People men an so lon again," We lov

and, w him ba he an rest in anothe for the has b wome up on likew anim and trees "Sav rest peo kee said of fear surrounding these gangs which prevents people with information coming forward but her statement is vital evidence in this case and we hope her strength will be an example for others to come forward too.

"We are determined to address the situation both on the Compton Estate and surrounding areas. Families should be able to feel safe and secure in their homes and children able to grow up in their local community without fear. That is the least they deserve."

It was also announced last night, as part of the crackdown being called Operation Enforcer, that Ellis Small another notorious local gang leader was arrested and held on a criminal charge of gang-related violence.

Dementia patients need saving drug

Reynolds

new developments show that - certain medicines are no
longer effective

The hou
A man h
with the
often beg
summer
close to t
people ,
The h
hard fac
has bee
after the
matche
happy
Ofter
comes
ment
housin
develo
have
built
comb
other

SEVEN YEARS LATER

Kaine watched his dad place the ring on his mum's hand. They were smiling at each other and everyone in the church was taking photos and filming them.

On their twentieth wedding anniversary, Daryll and Samantha Campbell were renewing their vows and Daryll had surprised Samantha by giving her another ring. It was a ring that Kaine, Roxy and Daryll had spent months trying to track down on the internet before they eventually found it and bought it back. It was Mamma's wedding ring.

'All right! Enough!' Kaine and Roxy both shouted out from the front row as their mum and dad started properly kissing each other.

They were laughing together, but then Kaine saw his sister turn towards AJ and hold his hand. 'Now don't you two start,' he said, wagging his finger.

He turned to the row behind him looking for some moral support, only to find that Mr K and Malin, each sitting with one of their red-haired twins on their laps, were also kissing each other.

'Oh my God,' said Kaine, throwing his hands up in the air. 'You're all at it!'

When the service was over, the congregation started to spill out of the church and onto the street. Kaine and Roxy were just catching up – they had so much to talk about – when a young boy who was reading the sports pages of the newspaper walked past them. Initially the boy just smiled at them and carried on his way.

Then he turned around and did a double-take, looking at the newspaper and then at Roxy and Kaine.

'It's you!' said the boy. 'It's *both* of you!' He ran up to them, thrusting the newspaper towards them. 'Will you both sign it for me?' he asked. 'Please?'

Roxy and Kaine smiled. 'Sure,' they said simultaneously.

CAMBELL TWINS EXCLUSIVE!

By **Claire Poulter**

Young stars open up on their journeys to success

UNSTOPPABLE

Kaine Campbell, the newly named PFA Young Player of the Year, has thanked his peers for the recognition and revealed that his inspiration comes from very close to home.

'My sister is my hero'

The youngster, who was originally spotted by legendary scout, Brian Hixon, burst onto the scene, scoring fifteen goals and assisting a further twelve in his breakthrough season. The Southampton midfielder was lauded by his fellow players at a star-studded event in London last night.

"I want to thank my family," said Campbell as he collected the award. "My gran was my inspiration and she still is. She taught me never to go for the ordinary. My mum and dad are my rocks. And my sister is my hero more and more every day. Together, I like to think we are unstoppable and my ambition is to get right to the top of my sport just like she has done.'

Kaine Campbell

Roxy Campbell x The Herald

Tennis's Dream Girl

Roxy Campbell has spoken of her joy after winning the Ladies' Wheelchair Singles Championship at Wimbledon to become the number one ranked player in the world.

The 21-year-old came back from a set down to win 3–6, 6–2, 6–1 and achieve a dream that, at one time, she was not sure she even wanted.

"I used to drive myself crazy"

"For a small part of my life, I wanted to escape tennis," Campbell admitted following her victory. "But when my life changed and I couldn't play, I realised how much I loved this game. I let myself miss it. I enjoyed missing it and I used that feeling as my driving force to get myself back on the court.

"When I was younger, I was so scared of not being perfect that I used to drive myself crazy with the fear of losing. But, after a while, I understood that I could never be perfect, and it was a like a weight being lifted off my shoulders. I just do my best and, if I'm lucky, like today, the ball listens to me and it's on my side."

An emotional Campbell also paid tribute to her father, Daryll. "When I won, I looked into the crowd and I could see my dad was clapping," she said. "Then he started crying and he set me off too. He and I have been on some journey and it hasn't always been perfect but that's ok. I've got my own coach these days, but I still want my dad with me whenever I play. Before a game, he always just comes in and gives me a hug and says the same words to me: 'Go do what you need to do.' That's all he says and it's all I need to hear. Just to know he's with me and he's proud of me. I'm proud of him too."

Kaine Campbell's

Left Foot

Rabona Goal

CAMPBELL OPENS THE DOORS

Roxy Campbell, the world number one wheelchair tennis star, today announced plans to open a brand new sports centre, which will provide opportunities, coaching and facilities for children with disabilities to learn and play a range of sports.

CAMPBELL
LENDS WEIGHT TO KNIFE CRIME BATTLE

Premier League star Kaine Campbell has become an ambassador for a charity formed to help fight knife crime. "Having Kaine involved is a huge boost to what we do," said Rufus Blackstock, a youth worker for the charity.

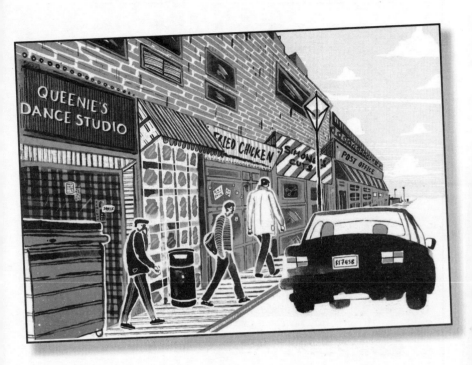

The Compton Academy

Message From The Principal, Mr Kerrigan and The Head of PE, Mr Campbell to all parents coming to watch school matches:

PLEASE REMEMBER
- Our students are young people
- This is a game
- The referee is human
- This is not a World Cup Final

Thank you and ENJOY the game!

Compton Academy

ACKNOWLEDGEMENTS

Firstly, thank you to my mum, Judy, and my stepdad, Ivan, for their love and support, always.

To Abi Sparrow and Philippa Perry of SP Agency for believing in me.

To David Fickling, Bella Pearson, Rosie Fickling, Phil Earle, Carolyn McGlone, Sabina Maharjan and the whole wonderful team at DFB for making me feel at home. It's a real privilege to work with you all.

To Steve and Lin Marshall for giving me the space and place to write.

And to the people who have been kind enough to help me on this journey: Lola Cashman, Matt Pauling, Alison Sturla, Lesley Minervini, Kate Thornton-Bousfield, William Bolitho, Les Reed, Clinton Coleman, Linda Hayes, Alastair Bennett, Doreen Kaye, Alison Gadsby, Susie Rickard, Tina Grant, Elaine McQuade, Cathy Hughes, Phil Smith, David Dein, Sue Cook, Sarah Stewart, Tamara Macfarlane, Noel Bradbury, Stuart Mawhinney, Martin Hitchcock, Ena McNamara, Mark Whittle, Joanne Whittle and Julie Ballard.

DAN FREEDMAN

READ THE ENTIRE JAMIE JOHNSON SERIES

There's only one Jamie Johnson